COWBOY PROTECTOR

Cowboy Confidential Book Two

LORI WILDE &
KRISTIN ECKHARDT

"Looks like we can cancel the funeral."

Hank Holden slowly opened his eyes, shifting on the bed and wincing at the bright sunlight streaming in through the ranch house window. Everything was fuzzy, making it hard for him to focus.

Huh?

His vision cleared and he saw three familiar faces staring down at him. "What am I doing here?"

"You took a hoof to the head, big brother," Cade Holden said, standing at the end of the bed. "I think that bull had it in for you. Maybe you're losing your touch as a veterinarian, Dr. Holden."

Sam Holden chuckled as he tipped up his cowboy hat. "Nah, it's cause Hank's getting old. You need faster men or slower cattle to get any work done around here."

"He's only thirty-five," Grandma Hattie countered, laying a gentle palm on Hank's cheek. "How are you feeling, dear?"

"Like I just got trampled by a half-ton bull."

"I'd call it a draw." Sam propped one cowboy boot on the bed frame. "That bull took quite a blow running into your hard head. But don't worry, he shook it off."

"Good to hear." Hank winced at the stabbing pain in his head. "And what are you doing here, Sam? I thought you were in El Paso."

"I just finished a job there and decided to stop by the ranch for a couple of days before I head out again."

Grandma Hattie reached out to give Sam a side hug. "I hope that's enough time for me to put some meat on your bones. I don't want you turning scrawny."

"No chance of that, Grandma." Sam pumped both arms in the air to show off his bulging muscles. "Now that Hank's down for the count, I'm the tough one in the family."

Hank half sat up in bed. "I can still kick your behind all the way to Laredo, if you'd like to try me."

Cade, the second youngest of the six Holden brothers, laughed as he grabbed Sam's arm and pulled him back. "Give Hank a break, Sam. He's got a mild concussion and some wounded pride. The doc said he needed take it easy."

"Wait, Dr. Culbertson was here?" Hank asked. The last thing he remembered was opening the cattle shoot, then everything went black.

"Yes, I thought it best to call him. He said that hoof just grazed you or it would have been a lot worse." Hattie reached out and gently smoothed the hair off Hank's forehead. "He was here a couple of hours ago. Don't you remember?"

"No, but I'm sure it will come back to me."

Worry furrowed her brow. "Do you know what day it is?"

He thought about it for a moment, trying to remember what day he'd promised to help work cattle. "Saturday?"

Grandma Hattie's face relaxed. "Yes, that's right."

Relieved, Hank leaned back against the down pillows, wincing at the movement. His body felt like one giant bruise and his head was pounding. Then he remembered there might be another reason for his condition—too many shots at the Wildcat Tavern last night with his business partner and fellow veterinarian, Charlie Dennison.

They'd shut down the place and he'd only gotten a couple of hours sleep before heading to the Holden family ranch to help work cattle this morning.

"Doc said you might not remember much around

the accident," Cade said. "He checked you over and didn't find too much damage. But he said you'd be mighty sore for a while."

Hattie nodded. "That's why I called Charlie. He's happy to cover your appointments at the vet clinic until you're fully recovered. And he told me you're overdue for a vacation anyway. It's perfect timing, really."

"Perfect...timing?" Hank said, feeling even more confused. Maybe his head wasn't quite as hard as his brothers thought.`

"For your job with Cowboy Confidential. We talked about it after the doctor left this morning." Hattie's blue eyes filled with concern. "Don't you remember?"

He didn't remember, but the last thing he wanted to do was make her worry. "It's...coming back to me..."

"Cowboy Confidential is real?" Sam interjected, staring at Hattie. "Nick told me you'd started a new business with that name, but I thought he was joking."

"It's as real as the honey buns baking in my oven right now," she said. "My own staffing company that I'm running right out of this house. And Nick knows that better than anyone, since working for Cowboy Confidential is how he met his fiancée."

All three brothers stared at their grandmother. Then Cade sputtered, "Nick's engaged? Since when?"

"Since yesterday." Hattie clasped her hands together, her face glowing. "He and Lucy called me last night to tell me the wonderful news." Then her blue eyes narrowed. "And it's about darn time one of you boys settled down. I can't wait forever to be a great-grandmother."

Hank cleared his throat. The last thing he wanted to settle down. "Did you say something about honey buns in the oven?"

"They'll be ready in about ten minutes," Hattie told him. "So that's plenty of time to talk about Cowboy Confidential."

Oh boy.

She pulled the bedcovers up around Hank's bare shoulders and then perched on the side of the bed. "It's doing even better than I imagined. I hired out your cousin Chet to work at a sale barn across town. Your uncle Brian took a job hauling a purebred Angus bull to a ranch in west Texas, and your cousin Katie agreed to create a software program for a horse breeder in Erath County. That girl is a whiz with computers."

Sam chuckled. "Sounds like you've put the entire Holden clan to work, Grandma."

"I plan to have plenty of work for anyone who wants it," Hattie said. "Now it's Hank's turn."

Hank was happy to help out his grandmother, just like he'd been doing since he was eleven years old. That's when his parents were killed in a car accident, leaving Hank and his brothers to be raised by their grandparents, Hattie and Henry Holden.

He still remembered the last words his father spoke to him before his parents left on that fateful weekend trip: *Take good care of your little brothers.*

And Hank had done just that, determined to fulfill that duty and make his late parents proud. He'd given up his childhood to work on Elk Creek Ranch and help out his grandparents, then paid his way through college and vet school so he could assist the family financially.

Now that Grandpa Henry was gone, he was often tempted to corral his ornery brothers, even though they were all adults now and living their own lives. But if any one of them ever needed Hank, he was there. And he'd always be there for Grandma Hattie too, no matter what she asked of him. "My turn for what...exactly?"

"Well, my friend Edith asked for my biggest, toughest grandson..."

"Hey," Cade and Sam protested in unison.

Hattie smiled at them. "You're all big, strong men, but Hank is the best fit for her job requirement. Maybe you two should have eaten more of my honey buns growing up, like your big brother." Then she turned back to Hank. "Anyway, Edith is looking for someone to stop a stalker."

"Edith has a stalker?" Hank had last seen Edith Cummings a few months ago when the petite septuagenarian had brought her cranky Siamese cat into his vet clinic for a wellness check.

"Oh, my no!" Hattie laughed. "Although she is on the hunt for a man. Her husband passed about ten years ago and she's ready to start dating again."

Hank closed his eyes and rubbed his forehead with his fingertips. "So what does Edith have to do with this job?"

"She's in a support group with a friend of the woman who's being stalked. Edith told her about Cowboy Confidential, so she and her friend contacted me. This stalker is after Dr. Rachel Grant, the therapist of the group."

He glanced over at his brothers, who looked as confused as he felt. "So this *Dr. Grant* wants me to protect her from a stalker?"

"Oh, no, Dr. Grant must *never* be told that her friends pitched in to hire you. Apparently, she's not that worried about the stalker. But everyone around her thinks she's not taking it seriously enough." Hattie leaned closer to him, her eyes twinkling. "So you'll need to go undercover as a mental patient."

The hoots of laughter from Sam and Cade didn't help his headache or his mood, but their amusement died down quickly enough with one stern glance from Grandma Hattie.

"A little therapy never hurt anyone," she told them. "And Sam, you're a bounty hunter, so you go undercover all the time. Didn't you once pretend to be a rodeo clown to catch some runaway felon?"

"Well, sure I did, but..."

"Hey, that's a good point," Hank interjected. "This sounds more like Sam's line of work than mine. I think he'd make a *perfect* mental patient. And if anyone in this family needs therapy, it's him."

"I've already got a job." Sam made a big show of looking at his watch. "In fact, I probably need to leave this afternoon just to get a good start. But I'll take the next Cowboy Confidential job you've got, Grandma. I promise."

The sound of chimes filled the room and Hattie stood up as she pulled her cell phone from her apron pocket and turned off the timer. "Oh, good, my honey buns are done. Sam, I'll pack up some for you to take on the road. And Cade, you need to confirm Hank's appointment with Dr. Grant."

"Monday morning at ten o'clock," Cade said, grinning at Hank. "Dr. Grant has a long waiting list, but I was lucky enough to get you in due to a cancellation."

Hank wanted to protest, but he knew once Grandma Hattie made up her mind about something, there was absolutely no changing it. He closed his eyes as they left the room, hoping sleep might numb the pain of his bruised body.

Then maybe he could dream about the fastest way to get out of this mess. Because the last thing he wanted was some nosy, highbrow therapist trying to psychoanalyze him. That meant he had to protect her, track down her stalker, and wrap up this job before she could sink her claws in too deep.

"I can't believe I let you talk me into another blind date!"

Rachel Grant strode into the ladies' restroom of the Pine City Bistro that evening with her best friend, Molly Loomis, right on her heels. The aroma of garlic and oregano wafted in after them, mingling with the floral air freshener in the tiny pink-and-white lavatory.

"I really thought you might like this one," Molly said as the swinging door closed behind her. A basket of toiletries sat on the sink top and Molly grabbed a bottle of scented lotion and poured a dollop into her palm.

"This is the last time," Rachel reminded her. "*You promised.*"

"C'mon, Rach. I know Tad is a little eccentric," Molly admitted as she rubbed her hands together.

"But he isn't that bad. Parker thought you two might make a good match."

"He's flossing his teeth at the table!"

"So he's got good hygiene habits. He's also into martial arts. I think that makes up for some of his other quirks."

"Like stealing that tip from the next table?"

"Actually I was talking about his toupee." Molly leaned toward the mirror, checking her flawless makeup. "I've never seen him wear it before, and believe me, he looks much better without it. Very distinguished. And he's one of the top salesmen at Parker's firm."

Groaning with frustration, Rachel turned away. She'd had it with her friends' attempts to fix her up with a man. She'd moved to Pine City from Philadelphia two years ago and had already been a bridesmaid twice. Now these same friends seemed determined to wrap her in white and shove her down the aisle.

For the past few months they'd besieged her with single men. Finally, Rachel had drawn the line, insisting that tonight be the last time either of them could play matchmaker. In her opinion, that was still one blind date too many, but a small penance to pay to keep her friends happy.

Unfortunately, Tad Grothen had proven just how far they were willing to go.

Molly had even dragged along her poor husband, Parker, for this disastrous double date. Now he was stuck out there watching Tad floss. Rachel loved her friends, but there were some things even she wouldn't do for them. And suffering through the rest of this date was one of them.

Rachel moved to the double-hung window, checking the dimensions. "It looks like a tight squeeze, but with a little luck and some body oil, I might be able to make it."

"What are you talking about?" Molly exclaimed. "You can't escape by climbing out the window. We're on the second floor of the restaurant!"

"I'm not going to escape. I'm planning to jump. It's definitely preferable to hearing more about Tad's disgusting toenail fungus."

"All right," Molly said with a resigned sigh. "I get your point. Maybe we have gone a little overboard with some of these guys. But we're worried about you...and you know the reason why."

Rachel sucked in a deep breath. "You don't need to worry. I've got it under control."

"I heard you received another one of those letters. The third one this week."

That's when Rachel knew Steven Doucette, the clinic's receptionist, had ratted her out. "I've shown the letters to the other three therapists at our clinic, so they're aware of them. Noah Lopez believes the writer is more obsessed with death than he is with me."

"And that's supposed to be reassuring?" Molly folded her arms across her chest. Her stint as a medic in the Air Force had taught her not to back down from anyone or anything. Now an emergency room doctor, her military training still showed in her ramrod straight back and the unflinching gaze of her hazel eyes. "And it's not just the letters. It's the fact that you live alone and don't have anyone watching out for you."

"I can take care myself," she assured her. "I've done pretty well so far."

"So what did this last letter say?"

Rachel sighed. *"If you live to be a hundred, I want to live to be a hundred minus one day, so I never have to live without you."*

"And what book is that from?"

"Winnie the Pooh."

Molly blanched. "And you don't find that just a little bit creepy?"

"It's harmless, just like all the other letters," Rachel told her. "They're probably from one of my blind dates who doesn't take rejection well. And Dr. Craig, our clinic director, did call in the police when the letters first started arriving, but nothing came of it. So, you really don't need worry; I've got it under control."

"I hope you're right."

"I am," she assured her. "And I'm happy. I'm single, okay? That's not something that needs to be fixed. All I want is for everybody to leave me and my love life alone."

"You don't have to pretend with me. You don't have a love life."

"And I'm not looking for one," she said, brushing stray bread crumbs off the skirt of her new topaz-blue dress. She'd loved this dress until Tad had told her his great aunt had one just like it.

"Is it because your heart's still broken?" Molly asked her. "You haven't seriously dated anyone since Russell dumped you."

Rachel stiffened. "He didn't dump me. He went on a sabbatical."

"Your fiancé left the country without even telling you! He's been gone for almost a year."

"We never officially broke up."

Molly rolled her eyes. "Does Russell write to you? Call you? Send you messages by carrier pigeon?"

"He's in a very remote part of Africa," Rachel replied. "Now I *really* don't want to talk about Russell. We just...grew apart."

"More than eight thousand miles apart."

Talking about him meant thinking about him, and that's the last thing Rachel wanted to do. "We should plan a girls' night soon."

Molly scowled. "You always do that."

"Do what?" Rachel asked.

"Change the subject whenever anyone brings up Russell."

"Most friends would take the hint."

"This friend is worried about you. Not only do you have a stalker, but I don't think you're as over your ex-fiancé as you pretend. It's like you're stuck in Russell limbo."

"You've been out of the dating loop for a while, Molly. It's not as easy to meet men when you get older."

"Oh, please." Molly rolled her eyes. "You're only thirty-two. If I had your gorgeous red hair, big green eyes, and knockout body, I'd have a date every night."

"Somehow I don't think your husband would approve."

But Molly wasn't ready to give up. "Just give Tad one more chance. He's probably done flossing by now. We can order dessert and see what happens."

"I already know what will happen. We'll be dodging chunks of chocolate ganache." Rachel glanced at her watch. "Besides, it's a been a long day. I saw patients this morning and I have a full schedule of appointments on Monday, followed by my Lonely Hearts group in the evening. I just need some downtime."

Molly arched a skeptical brow. "You want to go home alone at eight o'clock on a Saturday night?"

"Sounds like heaven to me."

"It sounds to me like you're still not over Russell." Molly shook her head. "I just don't get it, Rach. I know Russell's cute and that entomology is probably a respectable field. But what kind of man works with bugs all day? And didn't he have a cockroach collection?"

"Yes, with cockroaches from around the world. He wanted to display it in our living room after we were married. I voted for the garage."

Molly shivered. "That's so creepy. Can you imagine living with Russell and his dead cockroaches?"

"Not to mention his live gadfly collection. Which is another reason I'm so glad to be single." It was true. She had a great career. A nice apartment. A creepy pen pal.

"Speaking of cockroaches," Rachel said, "did you hear that Gina's husband left her for another woman? She wants to kill him. I mean, she's actually drawing up murder plans."

"Oh, no!" Molly exclaimed. "Well, I guess we all saw that coming. It's a good thing she's got a therapist for a best friend." Then she frowned. "Wait, you're doing it again—changing the subject."

"Actually, I'm forming my escape plan."

"You can't leave now. You're on a date!"

"My *date* has texted his mother three times in the last hour. She can have him." Rachel slung her purse over her shoulder. "I think I'll have more fun dealing with despair and depression at my group session on Monday night."

"I wish you'd worry as much about your stalker as you do about that Lonely Hearts group." Molly placed a hand on her shoulder. "I'm afraid for you, Rachel, even if you're not. I think having a man in your life would make you less vulnerable."

"Honey, I can take care of myself." Rachel reached out to give her hug. "But I appreciate the concern. And I promise to start locking my doors at night."

"Very funny."

"Look, this so-called stalker has never called me or left a message of any kind at my house. It's just these silly letters mailed to the clinic...and a few other minor incidents. For all we know, it's a prank by the dentists on the third floor."

Molly sighed. "I wish it was that simple. Just understand that I'd do anything—and I mean *anything*—to make sure you're safe."

"I know. But you promised me you won't fix me up with any more blind dates after tonight, remember?"

"I won't arrange any more blind dates," Molly affirmed, not quite meeting her gaze. "I promise."

"Good." Rachel smiled. "As I'm always telling my group, you don't have to be in love to be happy."

"And *you* don't have to sacrifice your love life to prove it to them."

"Believe me, with men like Tad around, it's no sacrifice." Rachel dug into her purse and pulled out some cash. "I've got to go. This should cover half the dinner bill."

"Don't leave," Molly pleaded. "I think Tad likes you. And I'm sure he's planning to ask you out again. What should I tell him?"

"Tell him I jumped out the window."

❧ 2 ☙

On Monday morning, Rachel spoke to the closed closet door in her office. "Only three more minutes, Mr. Kasper."

"I can't breathe," shouted a panicky voice from inside the closet. "I've got to get out of here!"

"Take slow, deep breaths," she replied in a calm, soothing tone. "Close your eyes and envision a safe place. Distract yourself by imagining you're in a cocoon."

"All right," came his shaky voice from the closet. "I'll...t...t...try."

"I know you can do this, Mr. Kasper." Rachel kept her fingers crossed. Jonathan Kasper was a new patient of hers, but he had been coming to the Craig Clinic for years.

A short, balding man on the brink of retirement,

he and his wife had big plans to travel around the world.

The only problem was he suffered severe attacks of claustrophobia every time he got on an airplane. He'd been making wonderful progress conquering his problem these past few weeks, but the acclimation phase was the most difficult part.

She glanced at her watch. This session was almost over and her new patient was due to arrive soon. Then she'd be free for a late lunch before the rest of her afternoon appointments.

She had a healthy salad waiting in the clinic lunch room, but there was a chocolate bar in the lobby vending machine calling her name.

Her office door cracked open, accompanied by a light knock.

"Yes?" she said, looking toward the door.

"Excuse me," intoned a deep, masculine voice. "There wasn't anyone at the reception desk. I'm looking for a Dr. Grant."

"You found her," she said as the door opened wider.

Then a cowboy stepped inside like he'd just walked off a movie set. He stood at least six four with a killer smile, the deepest blue eyes she'd ever seen, and dark whiskers shading his square jaw.

"You're Dr. Grant?" His brow furrowed as he

swept off his chocolate-brown Stetson and held it in one broad hand.

She smiled at the note of surprise in his voice. Maybe he wasn't expecting a woman. The clinic, started by renowned therapist, Dr. Roger Craig, had recently offered partnerships to three independent psychologists, including her.

"Yes, I'm Dr. Grant. And you are?"

"Your one o'clock appointment," he said. "I might be a bit early."

Her impotency case.

Rachel cleared her throat and took a deep breath, trying to hide her surprise. She was expecting someone older and less...magnetic.

But she knew better than anyone that appearances could be deceiving. And since she'd never had an impotency case before, she wasn't about to let this one get away. She put everything else out of her mind except making him comfortable.

"Welcome," she said, extending her hand toward him with an encouraging smile. "And your name is?"

"I'm Hank," he replied, clasping her hand in his big, warm callused one. A tingle shot through her arm as he gently squeezed her fingers.

His cocky, self-assured smile surprised her. She hadn't expected a man with such an easy, confident air.

On the outside he was built like a football lineman, with a handsome, square-jawed face and those heart-stopping blue eyes. But underneath that delectable exterior probably lay a sexually frustrated cowboy.

She could hardly wait to get her hands on him. Figuratively speaking.

Then she remembered that someone else had made that appointment for him, according to Steven, the clinic's receptionist. *His mother? Brother? Girlfriend?*

Her smile turned sympathetic as she realized her mistake. The confidence he exuded was probably a cover for the insecure man-child inside. The poor guy had even been too embarrassed to make the appointment himself. So better for her to take it slow and let *him* bring up his reason for being here.

"This is a little awkward," he began. "I'm not sure where to start..."

"Why don't we just take some time to get acquainted first?" She steered him toward the sofa. "That will make both of us more comfortable."

He sat down on the sofa and looked around the office. "I've never been to a place like this before."

"I hope it's not too scary," she said with a smile, walking over to the coffee station she kept in the corner of the room.

"I don't scare that easily."

So he liked playing the tough guy. That was called compensating.

"Please, just relax. I know why you're here," she said gently, "and I admire your courage in talking about something like this with a total stranger."

She hadn't expected a man so young, so attractive, so outwardly virile. The paradox intrigued her. He might make an interesting case study for the psychology book she wanted to write someday. Of course, she'd make certain his identity remained anonymous.

"Would you like a cup of coffee?" she asked, still sensing an air of uneasiness about him.

"Sure," he said, settling back against the sofa cushion with a slight wince.

Rachel kept her gaze on him as she picked up the coffee pot. "Are you all right?"

"It's nothing." He set his cowboy hat on the table beside him. "I just got banged up a bit yesterday working cattle."

He seemed determined to impress her. To prove his manliness. But he didn't need to convince her, he needed to convince himself. Impotency had nothing to do with masculinity or toughness.

Neither of them said a word as she poured the hot coffee into a white ceramic mug, although she could feel his steady gaze fixed on her. She blamed the fiery blush in her cheeks on the steam rising out of the coffee pot. "Do you take sugar or cream?"

"No, black is just fine."

"Shall I go first?" she asked, walking over to hand him the mug.

"Sure."

She sat in an armchair across from the sofa and kicked off her heels. Then she tucked her legs underneath her, unaware of the way her gray silk skirt rode up her thighs until she caught him staring at her legs.

"Hank? Are you with me?"

"What?" He looked up. "Oh. Right. Sure, go ahead."

Rachel cleared her throat. "Well, I grew up in Philly and attended Penn State University. That's where I got my master's degree in clinical psychology. Then I moved to Texas two years ago and earned my doctorate through North Texas University."

She hesitated, uncertain if she should relate more personal information. It seemed the least she could do, since he was about to divulge his most intimate secrets to her.

"I'm thirty-two years old and happily single," she continued. "Which still seems to shock my family. I collect antiques, and I am seriously thinking about getting a dog." Her life didn't sound too exciting, although he seemed quite interested. He leaned forward on the sofa, watching her intently as he sipped his coffee.

Time to get down to business.

"Are you single or married, Hank?"

"I'm single and like it that way."

She nodded. At least he didn't have to suffer from performance anxiety on a regular basis. "Do you date much?"

"Not as much as I'd like. I've been pretty busy with work these past few months."

"What do you do for a living?"

"I'm a country veterinarian, although I have quite a few small animal clients in Pine City too."

Rachel nodded. "Do you find yourself more comfortable with animals than people? Especially women? Is that why you've been avoiding more intimate relationships?"

He scowled. "I haven't been avoiding anything."

She leaned forward. "It's very natural, in our sessions, to be defensive at first. But I think you'll find it more helpful to be reflective. To listen, instead of instantly reacting. And take time to really think about what I'm saying to see if it might resonate with you."

He sat there for a long moment; his skeptical gaze locked on her. At last he said, "I. Haven't. Been. Avoiding. Anything."

Hmm, she needed to take a different approach.

Men like Hank didn't react well to a soft touch—he wanted to battle. "Okay, let me ask you another question."

"Shoot," he said, taking a long sip of his coffee.

"Do you suffer from premature ejaculation?"

He spit coffee halfway across the room. "*What?*"

"I know impotency and sexual dysfunction are very sensitive subjects," she said quickly, watching as Hank reared up off the sofa, "but it's better to face them head-on."

He slammed the mug on the coffee table "I don't think you understand, lady."

"Doctor."

"Okay, *Doctor*. I came here to talk about something else. Something else *entirely*."

"Hank, listen..."

"Doctor," he corrected her. "Dr. Hank Holden."

"Doctor," she said, trying to hide her smile. Expressing his anger was a good sign and the first step to digging into the rest of his deeply buried emotions.

Yes, he would make an excellent subject to study for her future book. And as she watched him start to pace, stalking back and forth like a caged animal, a possible title popped into her mind: *Feral Men and the People Who Love Them*.

"We can talk about whatever you'd like," she said, hoping to calm him. "I'm here to help you. Impotence can often be a complex problem, so there are many layers to probe. Once the physical reasons have been ruled out, we can turn to more intensive therapy."

He stopped pacing and stared at her, the color draining from his face. "I don't need any therapy or probing. Intensive or otherwise."

Rachel swallowed. She had the distinct feeling she wasn't handling this as well as she'd hoped. "It can be very beneficial in cases like yours..."

"Hold it," he insisted. "There is no case. I only came here because of your friends..."

"What?" Rachel suddenly realized she'd been wrong. This man didn't suffer from a lack of confidence. Just the opposite, in fact.

And she suddenly had a nagging suspicion he didn't suffer from impotency, either.

The closet door suddenly crashed open, shaking the walls in her small office. Hank whirled around and barreled toward Mr. Kasper.

"Wait!" Rachel cried.

But it was too late. Hank tackled the older man to the ground. Mr. Kasper let out a gasp of surprise as his back end hit the carpeted floor and Hank pinned the man's shoulders to the ground.

"Let go of him!" Rachel demanded. "What are you doing?"

"Saving you," Hank snapped. "Now call the police."

"Can I just go back in the closet?" Mr. Kasper asked, his face pale and dripping with sweat. Then he looked up at Hank and did a double take. "Dr. Holden? Well, my goodness, this *is* a surprise."

Hank's fierce expression relaxed and he helped Mr. Kasper to his feet. "Sorry about that, Jon. I didn't recognize you without your Texas Rangers cap on."

"No problem," Jon said, brushing himself off.

Rachel hurried toward the older man. "I'm so sorry, Mr. Kasper. Are you all right?"

"I think I'm good. It got pretty hot in that closet." Then he grinned, mopping his damp brow with his white handkerchief. "Sounds like it got pretty hot out here, too."

She vigorously fanned him with a mental health journal, mortified that she'd neglected one of her patients. "I can't believe you stayed in there for so long."

"I think I'm cured," he announced. "You were right about finding a distraction, Dr. Grant." He rubbed his hands together. "Yes, indeed. That makes all the difference in the world."

She swallowed. "Mr. Kasper, you realize that anything you might have overheard between Dr. Holden and I is strictly confidential. He's a patient of mine..."

"I am *not* your patient," Hank countered, before she could explain any further.

Mr. Kasper shook out the limp handkerchief and then stuffed it in his pocket. "So that means the confidentiality rules don't apply?"

She opened her mouth, but Hank answered first. "Of course not. I've never even met Dr. Grant before today. And this is the first time I've ever been in a therapist's office in my life."

Mr. Kasper lifted his orange Longhorns jacket off the coatrack. "Well, I've got to run. I can't wait to tell Thelma all about my day."

Rachel struggled to maintain her composure. "I'm sure your wife will be thrilled you've finally overcome your claustrophobia."

Mr. Kasper grinned. "Yes, that, too." He zipped up his jacket as he headed for the door. Then he turned to Hank. "And don't worry, Doc, I'll make certain the paper doesn't print anything about..." He lowered his voice to a whisper. "*Your little problem.*"

After he left, Hank slowly turned to face her. "The paper? What exactly did he mean by that?"

She folded her arms across her chest, deriving a certain satisfaction from his stricken expression. "Didn't you know Mr. Kasper's sister-in-law is Midge Berman? She writes the daily gossip column for the Pine City Herald and recently became the host of a local talk show called *Pine City People*."

He closed his eyes. "I don't believe it."

"I tried to warn you." She experienced a twinge of remorse. "I'm sorry. I completely forgot he was in there."

His eyes flew open. "How could you possibly forget a man in your closet?"

Not certain of the answer herself, she shrugged. When Hank had walked into her office, all her common sense seemed to have vanished. "I know why you're really here."

"You do?"

She nodded. "My friends have been worried about me because I've been getting odd, unsigned letters in the mail. The letters are benign, but I understand their concern. For some reason, they think I need to have a man in my life to protect me—or save me, as you so aptly put it."

When Hank didn't deny it, she continued. "So they somehow talked you into making an appointment with the intention of dating me? Even though that's completely unethical." She shook her head. "I apologize. I believe it's cruel to lead someone on or give them false hope. That's why I want to be honest with you."

Hank stayed silent.

Rachel studied his face but couldn't read his expression. Many people didn't handle rejection well, so she wanted to let him down easy. "I don't think you're the man for me, Dr. Holden. Frankly, after a raft of blind dates, I'm not interested in dating anyone at the moment."

"Good to know."

Thank heavens. She was glad to see he was taking her friends' elaborate ruse so well. "I'm curious, though. Why was this scheduled as an impotency issue?"

He hesitated. "My brother was actually the one who scheduled it. He made a big mistake."

"Oh," she replied, surprised but not wanting to push the matter. "Well, let me walk to you to the door."

Hank picked up his cowboy hat and followed her across the room. "Sorry about tackling Jon. I hope he's okay."

"I think he will be." She smiled as she opened the door for him. "Good luck to you, Dr. Holden."

"Thank you, Dr. Grant." He took a long look at her before walking out the door. "I'm going to need it."

❧ 3 ❧

"And she said I'm not the man for her."

Charlie Dennison shook his head as he stared at the television screen. "Unbelievable." Then he jumped to his feet and shouted, "Block the lane! Block the lane!"

Hank found it difficult to focus on the Mavericks game, although he loved basketball. He and Charlie always got together at Hank's house to watch sports on his big screen. But tonight Hank's mind kept drifting back to his meeting with Dr. Rachel Grant.

She was impossibly stubborn and impossibly beautiful—especially when she was angry. Not that he'd made her angry on purpose, but the sparks he'd seen in those bewitching green eyes still made him feel a little woozy.

Or maybe that was his concussion.

His dog, Georgie, padded over to him, then leaped onto the black leather recliner and draped herself across his lap. The German shorthaired pointer had been by his side almost every moment since he'd returned from his disastrous counseling appointment with Rachel.

His dog always seemed to know when he was hurting—but he wasn't sure if Georgie was sensing his physical injuries from the bull or the blow to his ego.

"Why would she think I'm not that man for her," Hank said aloud, still perplexed that Dr. Grant seemed immune to his charms. He'd never gotten that kind of reaction from a woman before.

"Pass it!" Charlie yelled.

Georgie started gently licking one of the many bruises on Hank's forearm, leading him to softly stroke the top of her head to reassure her. "It's okay, girl. I'm fine."

Georgie looked up at him with her soulful brown eyes, as if she didn't quite believe him, then rested her head against his chest.

"He's open! He's open," Charlie shouted at the television, then raised both arms straight in the air in celebration. "Three points!"

"Yes, as if he can hear you."

Charlie turned to Hank as the game went to

commercial. "So this therapist turned you down? Was this before or after she called you impotent?"

"After." Hank reached into the bowl of peanuts on the table beside him. "I'm sure Cade had big laugh about it when he made that appointment. But we'll see whose laughing when I'm through with him."

"That might take a few months considering your condition. Although I notice your face is untouched, so I'm a little surprised the woman turned you down." Charlie grinned. "That's new for you, isn't it?"

"Rachel is...different."

"Oh, you're calling her Rachel now? Wow, she did get in your head."

Grandma Hattie stepped into the living room, drying her hands with a dish towel. Nacho, his orange tabby cat, was right on her heels. "I heard some yelling in here. Did you need boys something?"

"No, Grandma, we're fine. Charlie and I were just talking about the game." He didn't want her to know he'd struck out the first day on the job. Especially since she was the one who had taught him never to quit when things got tough.

She nodded. "Okay, well, supper will be ready soon. I'll plate it up for you boys so you can eat out here and watch the game."

"You don't have to do that," Hank said, knowing his protest would be useless. Grandma Hattie did exactly what she wanted, when she wanted. And currently, she wanted to treat Hank like he was still a little kid.

"Oh, it's no bother," Hattie said. "Do you need another ice pack?"

"Nope, this one's still good." Hank reached back to shift the ice pack to a different spot on his shoulder.

He was even more sore today than he'd been yesterday, with new bumps and bruises surfacing all over his body. But if he had to choose between the bull and Rachel, he'd almost rather face down the bull again.

Too bad that wasn't an option.

"One more thing, Grandma Hattie," Hank asked. "We never discussed how long this job is supposed to last. Or maybe we did, but I don't remember."

"Well, Rachel's friends paid for two weeks of services." A glint of pride shone in her blue eyes. "I even told them it might not take that long, because once Hank Holden sets his mind to something, he gets it done."

"No pressure there," Charlie said under his breath as Hattie disappeared down the hallway.

Hank didn't mind working under pressure, but this job didn't involve vaccinating a herd of cattle or treating an injured horse or any one of a hundred challenging jobs that he'd taken on over the years.

It involved Dr. Rachel Grant, who had made it

perfectly clear that he wasn't the man for her. So how could he change her mind?

Charlie sighed. "I wish your grandmother would come to my place every day and fix me supper. And dust. And vacuum. And do my laundry."

"She only does it when one of us is sick or injured." Hank started to shrug his shoulders, but the pain stopped him. "It's like she takes personal afront to any germ or mishap that dares to harm one of her grandsons. And it's not like we have a choice. Believe me, I'd rather she just take it easy now that Grandpa's gone. Instead, she's started a new business."

Charlie grinned. "And convinced you to take on a job for her during your vacation time. She seems like one smart lady to me."

"And I'm not going to let Grandma Hattie down. One way or another, I'm going to protect Rachel from her stalker."

"Sounds like Dr. Grant's not interested in your services. It's funny how you can't stop talking about her though."

Hank scowled. "That's not true."

"You haven't talked about anything else, including the game, since I walked through the front door." He looked at the dog. "Back me up, Georgie."

But Georgie just snoozed peacefully on Hank's lap, apparently unconcerned about the recent complications in Hank's life.

"So she's really a knockout?" Charlie asked.

"Yeah," Hank said, then cleared his throat. "But that's not relevant. Some creep out there must think she's a knockout too, which is why he won't leave her alone. So how do I find him and protect her at the same time?"

"Especially since she's already rejected you." Charlie smirked. "Sorry, I've just never heard of that happening to Dr. Love 'em and Leave 'em before, so I'm going to enjoy it for a while."

Even Hank couldn't remember the last time a woman had turned him down. And he sure didn't like the way it made him feel: frustrated, confused, and worst of all, helpless. "I just need to get Rachel to listen to me."

Grandma Hattie entered the room carrying a large serving tray with two plates on it filled to the brim. "I know how to make that happen."

Hank wondered if his grandma had been eavesdropping in the hallway. He hoped so, because he could use some help right now. "How?"

"Go to Dr. Grant's group meeting tonight. The one Edith attends every week. It starts at eight o'clock and they each get a turn to talk about anything they want. Maybe you can convince her to give you another chance."

Hank stared at her as she set the plates on the

coffee table. "Do you mean that Lonely Hearts group?"

"That's the one," she said, handing him some utensils. "I made pizza, wings, and some homemade queso for the chips, so have it, boys. And there's more where that came from."

He checked his watch, surprised to see that it was almost quarter till eight. He jumped up, dislodging Georgie from his lap, then almost cried in pain from the sudden movement. It took a moment for his head to stop spinning.

The dog gracefully leaped onto the floor and pranced with excitement.

"Sorry, girl," Hank said, leaning down to scratch her behind the ears, "but we're not going for a walk right now. Charlie will take you out soon, won't you, Charlie?"

"Sure." Charlie looked up in surprise, a chicken wing in each hand. "But where are you going?" Then a light dawned in his eyes and he grinned. "Oh, you're going after Dr Grant, aren't you? But don't you want to finish watching the game first?"

"Nope." Hank grabbed his cowboy hat before heading for the door. "I've got a game of my own to play."

Rachel couldn't be more pleased as she sat with the small circle of people gathered in her office. She'd started her Lonely Hearts group only a couple of months ago, but they were already bonding. And the newest member, her friend Gina Mitchell, seemed to fit right in.

In less than fifteen minutes, Gina learned about Edith's exploration with a new dating app, Frank's desire to find a woman who liked fishing as much as he did, and Lacie's distress at her ex-boyfriend's news that he was bunking with a new cowgirl.

Rachel just sat back and observed the group dynamics, watching as Gina sat cross-legged on the green tweed sofa in her office, dressed in loose, gray sweatpants and an oversized Texas Tech sweatshirt.

Her curly dark hair was pulled back into a loose ponytail and she stopped wearing mascara because it made crying messier. Rachel knew Gina had been insecure about men, so Kurt's straying had cut deep.

"So then he dumped me," Gina explained, her nail-bitten fingers picking apart the empty paper coffee cup in her hands. "For some older woman with fake boobs, fake hair extensions, fake everything."

"Then your future ex-husband can look forward to a fake relationship," Edith said, "and you can live authentically, knowing that you haven't betrayed someone you loved."

"Oh, he's going to be sorry to lose me," Gina

promised, walking over to the trash can to toss the shredded remnants of the coffee cup away. "The funny thing is that Kurt doesn't even seem like my husband anymore. It's as if someone else is inside of him, pulling all his strings."

"Like an alien in a Kurt suit?" Edith said, laughing. "That reminds me of *Men in Black*, one of my favorite movies. And that Tommy Lee Jones is a hottie!"

Rachel had seen *Men in Black* enough times to know every line. The cockroach scenes alone had made it one of Russell's favorite movies. She was just happy to see her group bonding so well and they were certainly more entertaining than any of her recent blind dates. Now she couldn't floss her teeth without thinking about Tad.

Her mind drifted to the nicer memory of Hank walking into her office this morning. She couldn't imagine dating a cowboy like him, although just the thought of it made her feel a little wobbly inside.

Part of her was relieved that his appointment was a ruse, because the way she'd been thinking about him was *anything* but professional.

"Thinking that Kurt has been taken over by an alien does make me feel better," Gina said with a smile. "Although our wedding anniversary is coming up soon, so that's something to dread."

Everyone groaned in unison, then Lacie said, "I hate special dates now, like anniversaries, holidays,

LORI WILDE & & KRISTIN ECKHARDT

or even my birthday. They're just not as fun anymore."

"That's why I wanted to join your group, because I knew you'd understand." Gina rubbed her forehead. "I just feel like I'm too old to start over. I don't even want to think about dating again. I'm used to being Mrs. Kurt Kurtz."

"Wow, that's quite a name," Frank said, shaking his head. "I have to believe you're not sorry to get rid of that."

"No, you're right," Gina said. "There are some bright spots to this divorce. They're just really hard to see sometimes."

"There's no hurry to start dating again," Lacie told her. "I'm taking my sweet time. And you seem to be handling your husband dumping you pretty well, all things considered."

"Not really. If Rachel hadn't talked me out of lacing his coffee with rat poison, I'd be sitting in a jail cell right now. But she knew just how I felt, after what she'd been through with Russell."

Three pairs of eyes turned in Rachel's direction.

"Who's Russell?" Lacie asked.

Edith leaned forward in her chair. "Were you married, Dr. Grant?"

Frank just stared at her, his mouth hanging open. At last he said, "I thought you were a lesbian."

Rachel made a mental note to lace Gina's coffee

with rat poison. "No, I'm not married and I'm not a lesbian. But we're not here to talk about me."

"Russell was her fiancé," Gina explained to the group. "He just up and left her without a word last year on Valentine's Day. Isn't that despicable?"

"I don't want to waste part of the group's time talking about me," Rachel said, wondering how she could steer the group to another topic. But maybe that wasn't fair. They were sharing all their lonely heart stories, so why should she get a pass?

"I think it's just awful," Lacie exclaimed. "Dumping someone on the most romantic day of the year?"

"What's so romantic about it?" Edith asked. "Valentine's Day is just an annual reminder that I'm old and alone."

"Valentine's Day is a week from tomorrow," Rachel said. "How does everyone feel about that?"

"Lonely," Frank replied. A retired feed salesman, he now spent his days on a fishing boat. When his wife filed for divorce eight months ago, she'd listed 'alienation of affection to a wide-mouth bass' as one of her reasons.

Lacie cupped her chin in her palm. "It makes me feel like a loser." At just twenty-two years old, Lacie had joined the group a month ago.

Dressed in a black tunic sweater and matching jeans, her hot-pink cowboy boots were hard to miss.

The daughter of a rancher, she worked as a waitress and was still trying to figure out what she wanted to do with her life.

"I say we boycott Valentine's Day," Edith proclaimed. "I mean, it's not like I have a date for it anyway."

"So how would this boycott work?" Frank asked. "Would we picket somewhere?"

Edith shook her head. "No, that's too much work. We just need to find a way to make a statement that Valentine's Day doesn't have to be celebrated—and that it often causes great unhappiness for many people."

"Or maybe we could have a personal boycott of the day by not getting caught up in the hype," Rachel suggested. "Instead of celebrating romantic love, you could celebrate loving yourself."

"But I want to do more than love myself," Gina replied, looking wistful. "I want to feel normal again. Right now, I feel like I'm on a roller coaster ride of anger and sadness." Then she looked over at Rachel. "How do I get off the roller coaster?"

Rachel had been asking herself that question ever since Russell had left her. Sometimes she wondered if she would ever heal.

"There are no easy answers," Rachel told group. "I once read that unhappiness comes from our resistance to accept reality. We want things to be different and the fact that they aren't makes us feel angry or sad or resentful."

"So I shouldn't be angry that Kurt left me?" Gina asked, looking confused.

"Of course you can be angry. You need to feel those emotions to process them." Rachel saw Edith nod in agreement. "But once you reach acceptance of what *is*, then you can start to heal and move forward."

"Wow," Lacie said. "I wish I was as cool as you, Dr. Grant. I've done so many stupid things since my boyfriend broke up with me."

Rachel smiled. "I'm not cool at all, Lacie. In fact"—she looked around the group—"I'll tell you a secret I've never told anyone."

"Not even me?" Gina asked in surprise.

"Not even you," she admitted. "When my fiancé ran off last year, he broke my heart. I was so hurt and embarrassed that I didn't tell anyone he'd left." She took a deep breath. "I even sent myself flowers on Valentine's Day and pretended they were from Russell, just to avoid any awkward questions. And I wrote myself a beautiful note to go with the flowers."

No one said anything for a long moment, then Gina pressed one hand against her chest and gave a relieved laugh. "Oh, that makes me feel so much better. Maybe I'm not crazy after all."

"I know!" Lacie exclaimed, her face brightening.

"If Dr. Grant can do something like that, then maybe it's normal to feel this way."

Rachel held up her hands. "Hold on, I don't believe that any one person should be the definition of normal. We're all on a spectrum. There's no right way or wrong way to be."

"Does that mean it's not wrong to want to kill my husband?" Gina mused. "Because I think I'd really enjoy killing him. I've thought of so many ways to do it."

"If you need to get rid of the body," Frank offered, "I've got a boat over at Callahan's Lake. The water's pretty deep there."

For a moment, everyone just stared at Frank until the older man finally burst out laughing. "I'm just joking, ladies. That lake's not deep enough to hide a body."

"Instead of planning a murder, let's play true confessions," Edith suggested. "Dr. Grant has already started us off. We'll all tell one embarrassing secret that we've been ashamed to admit before."

Before Rachel could respond, she heard footsteps behind her and turned to see Hank Holden walk into her office.

"Hi, I'm Hank," he said with a wave. "Am I in time to join your Lonely Hearts Club?"

"You're here to join our *club*?" Rachel asked archly.

"Yes, if you'll have me." Hank was still trying to catch his breath as he walked into her office. The ten-mile trip into Pine City from his acreage outside of town had been delayed by a flat tire.

He'd changed it and had his pickup truck back on the road in record time, breaking a few speed limits on the way. But now he was late, his stomach was growling, and his headache was back with a vengeance.

He feared his strategy might have backfired. Because Dr. Rachel Grant did *not* look happy to see him. The way his luck was running tonight, she'd probably think he was her stalker.

But it was too late to back out now.

"Of course we'll have you!" Edith rose to her feet to greet him. "We're not a club exactly, but that sounds more fun than a therapy group."

"I'm Frank," an older man said, pulling an empty chair into the circle. "Have a seat, Hank. It will be nice to have another man in the club. I was feeling outnumbered."

"And you already know me," Edith said, beaming at him as he sat down. She resumed her seat and told the group, "Hank is the grandson of a dear friend of mine. He's a veterinarian. And a bachelor!"

As Edith made the introductions, he noticed another familiar face in the circle.

"So what are you doing here, Dr. Holden?" Lacie asked him with a bemused smile. "Don't tell me you have a lonely heart. On the weekends, I waitress at the Wildcat Tavern and I always see you there with a woman on your arm. Usually, a different woman every time."

Hank chuckled. "Hey, Lacie, isn't there some kind of waitress and patron confidentiality agreement? I don't want you spilling all my secrets."

Lacie laughed. "I won't tell on you if you don't tell on me."

"Deal," Hank said, glancing at Rachel.

He still couldn't believe what he'd overheard before making his presence known—Dr. Rachel Grant's fiancé had abandoned her a year ago on Valentine's Day. He suddenly felt a surge of anger. What kind of jerk would do that to a woman like her? Or to any woman?

Lacie had been right to call him out on his active dating life, but he'd never made any promises that he couldn't keep.

"We were just about to share our secrets, Dr. Holden," Rachel told him with a cool smile. "Since you're new here, we'll let you go first."

He shifted in his chair, not expecting to be put on the spot. Yet, he sensed this was some kind of test. Maybe if he passed, she'd learn she could trust him. "I have so many secrets, it's hard to choose just one."

Everyone laughed except Rachel. Her gaze was fixed on him and he knew a challenge when he saw one. If he backed down now, he'd lose any opportunity he might have to help her.

"Okay," he said at last. "I do have a secret that I've never shared with anyone."

As the group stared expectantly at him, Hank was suddenly hit with an urge to make something up. But he was in too deep now and he'd never been a coward, so he took a deep breath and plowed ahead with the truth. "My secret is...that I've never been in love."

"What?" Gina gasped. "How is that possible? You're at least thirty..."

"Thirty-five," Hank said. "And I don't know if it's unusual or not, but it's true." He held up both hands. "Don't get me wrong, I love women. I mean, I *really* love women. But I've just never been *in* love with a woman before."

He found himself looking over at Rachel to gauge her reaction and was surprised to find that she looked intrigued. Maybe his strategy was working after all.

Frank scratched his grizzled chin. "But it sounds like you've got the ladies falling at your feet. So why join our club?"

"Yes," Rachel agreed, tapping a pen against the notepad on her lap. "I'm wondering the same thing."

Hank realized he hadn't thought that far ahead,

but before he could make up a credible reason for joining them, someone answered for him.

"Isn't is obvious?" Edith said with a fond glance at Hank. "We're all here because we've loved someone deeply—and then lost them. But Hank's here because he doesn't even know what that kind of love feels like." Tears shimmered in her brown eyes. "And that must be the loneliest feeling in the world."

4

After the group session was over, Hank chatted in the lobby of the office building with the group members until he was the last one there. Then he walked back to Rachel's office.

Looking through the open doorway, he saw her standing at the front of her desk. Her back was to him and her palms were planted on the desktop, as if trying to hold herself up. She now wore a light-blue trench coat over her gray suit and her black leather purse was on the floor beside her, as if she'd suddenly dropped it there.

Something didn't feel right.

Was she angry about him crashing the group? Or did bringing up memories of her ex-fiancé explain her strange posture and the heavy silence in the room?

Was that the reason she'd formed the Lonely Hearts group? To deal with her own loss and heartbreak?

He'd been ready to march into her office and make his case once more, but now he hesitated. What could he possibly say? She knew he didn't have any problem with impotence or finding women to date, so she'd question why he was there. And he couldn't tell her the real reason—that he'd been hired to protect her—because he'd given his word to Grandma Hattie.

Hank shook himself. He usually didn't hesitate to act, but something was holding him back. Maybe it was his concussion, which still throbbed in the back of his head. Or the fact that Rachel seemed immune to his charms. The reason didn't matter, he had a job to do.

"May I come in?" he asked.

She slowly turned around, her face pale and drawn. "What are you still doing here?"

"We need to talk."

She looked him up and down, then squared her shoulders. "All right, come in."

He walked inside, composing his argument in his mind while closing the distance between them in just a few strides. But when he reached her, his plan evaporated. "What's wrong?"

"I have a stalker." She cleared her throat. "And he's escalating. I don't know why I'm telling you this, other than I feel like I need to tell someone in case..."

"In case something happens to you?" he finished for her.

Rachel nodded, then met his gaze. "I'm probably overreacting, but I found this in my pocket just now."

She picked up a piece of black-rimmed notepaper from her desk and handed it to him.

Hank looked at the typewritten words. "Is this supposed to be a poem?" Then he read it aloud *"I send you no flowers, nor sweet candy hearts. But I'll never leave you, 'til death do us part."*

Hank noticed the fold line in the middle of the note. He turned it over, but the other side was blank.

"This is different than the letters," Rachel said, filling the silence. "This one is typed instead of hand-written. And a poetic verse instead of a quote from literature."

"And with an implied threat," Hank growled. "*'Til death do us part?* He sounds like a psycho."

"I wonder if Valentine's Day coming up has triggered an escalation," she mused. "It seems to have triggered some of our group members into considering a boycott."

Hank watched her mouth press into a thin line and could see that she was almost shaking. "Hey, it's all right." He awkwardly patted her shoulder. "Anyone would be scared to receive something like this."

"Scared? I'm not scared, I'm furious. Mostly with myself for not taking action sooner."

"What action?"

She raked her hands through her hair, dislodging silky red tendrils from her neat bun. They curled around her cheeks and bounced as she began to pace back and forth across the office.

"Until yesterday, I assumed whoever was sending me those letters was a current or former patient who had developed feelings for me. It's called transference and it's fairly common in my profession."

"So what happened yesterday?"

She stopped pacing and turned to face him. "When I begin therapy with a new patient, I usually have them handwrite a letter from their happier future self. It's a motivational tool to help them move toward the positive changes they want to make in their lives."

"Okay," Hank said slowly. "But I'm not sure I get the point."

"I make a copy of each of those future letters and keep them in my files. So I compared the handwriting of my stalker to all my patients' letters, but none of them matched."

Hank nodded. "You're saying it's likely that your stalker *isn't* one of you patients?"

"That's right. And I know he lives in or near Pine

City, because the letters he sent were postmarked from here."

"And how can you be certain it's a man?"

Rachel walked over to her file cabinet and retrieved a folder from one of the drawers. "Because of the quotes he sent me. A few of them refer to a man's love for a woman. It's never the other way around."

"That folder is awfully thick. How long has this guy been contacting you?"

"For about the past six months or so. The letters were pretty infrequent at first, but lately I've been getting several a week." She nibbled her lower lip. "I wonder if something's changed for him to make direct contact like this. Either Valentine's Day or something in his personal life or..."

"Don't you think it's more important to figure out *how* he got that note into your coat pocket," he said, amazed by her composure, "before you worry about his motivation?"

"Oh, I already figured that out. The only opportunity for him to have access to my coat was this morning at Bonnie's Diner, where I stopped for breakfast. I'm a regular customer there and they have a coatrack near the door."

"So he probably knows your routine." Now Hank began to pace, worried that Rachel was in more danger than anyone had imagined. Her friends had been right; she truly did need protection. "Which means he's been following you and could know where you live."

"I'm sure he does."

If she was scared, she didn't show it, which Hank thought was either incredibly brave or incredibly naive. Either way, they had to take action. "I think we should call the police. My brother Nick is a detective and..."

"No," she said briskly. "I talked to a police officer when I first started receiving the letters, but there's really nothing they can do until he actually threatens me. And I don't even know who it is."

"Well, anyone who would do this is nuts!"

"We don't use the terms *nuts* or *psycho* in my profession, but the man obviously needs help." Then she smiled up at him. "And that's where you come in."

"How, exactly?" Was she about to ask him to protect her until this lunatic could be identified? That would certainly make his job easier.

Rachel reached up to smooth her loose hair, pinning the stray tendrils neatly back into place. "Since he's obviously been watching me, that means he's knows I'm single and live alone." She took a step closer to Hank. "So I need a way to flush him out."

He bit back a smile. "Does this mean you'll..."

"Start dating you? No." Then Rachel held up one

hand. "Let me clarify. I want us to *pretend* that we're dating. To be madly in love, actually."

"Madly in love?"

She grabbed his hand and pulled him out the door of her office and into the empty, well-lit lobby, not stopping until they reached the big plate glass window near the entrance. A crescent moon adorned the night sky.

"What are we doing?" he asked her.

"If my stalker is following me, he's now got a perfect view of us through this window." She moved closer to Hank and looped her slender arms around his neck. "I want you to kiss me."

"What?" The way her soft, supple body pressed lightly against his made him feel a little dizzy. "Now?"

"Right now," she whispered, her warm breath caressing his mouth. "Kiss me like you really mean it."

Rachel thought she was ready to be kissed by Hank Holden, but the moment his mouth captured hers, she realized she was in way over her head.

Because Hank didn't just kiss her. He wrapped his strong arms around her and pulled her into his large rock-solid body in a full-fledged assault on her senses. She felt his thick shoulder muscles flex beneath her fingertips and heard the low, guttural moan in his throat. He tasted like honey and made her forget everything but the man in her arms.

Suddenly, a car blasted its horn as it passed by the window, startling them both. Hank abruptly released her and she took a step back from him, wondering what had just happened. He'd kissed her with an intensity she'd never experienced before. Certainly not with Russell. She'd always thought Russell was a good kisser, but he'd *never* kissed her like that.

Her face warmed when she remembered telling Hank to kiss her like he really meant it. Too bad it was just part of a ruse.

"Do you think that was him?" he asked, breaking her reverie.

She blinked up at him. "What?"

"The car that just honked at us. Do you think that was your stalker?"

"Oh." Rachel peered out the large window, but the dark street was mostly empty. "I have no idea."

"It looked like a white Ford Taurus when it passed under the streetlight, but I didn't catch the license plate number."

Her excitement over the best kiss of her life started to fade when she realized it hadn't fazed Hank at all. While she'd been melting in his arms, he'd been checking the cars driving by outside. She took another step back from him, trying to regain her equilibrium. "I can't think of anyone I know who drives a white Ford Taurus, but I'll make a note of it."

He nodded. "So what's our next step?"

That was a good question. The kiss had been an impulse of the moment, driven by her need to discover who had left that note in her coat pocket. She'd wanted to draw the attention of her stalker and it may have actually worked. Or else the driver of that Taurus just appreciated the show they'd put on through the window.

Heat burned in her cheeks as she looked up at Hank, wondering what he was thinking. Had he even wanted to kiss her? A twinge of guilt rippled through her at the way she was using him to catch her stalker. But maybe she could make it worth his while.

She squared her shoulders, determined to put that kiss behind her. "Hank, I have a proposition for you."

"Absolutely not."

Hank sat across from her in Bonnie's Diner, looking more stubborn than usual. The vintage diner had been a staple in Pine City for close to eighty years and was located only a few blocks from her clinic. They specialized in breakfast food, but served a full menu at all hours of the day or night.

"I'm happy to help," he told her, "but I won't take a penny from you."

It was just past ten p.m., but the 24-hour diner was busy with take-out orders and customers kept filling the red padded stools at the lunch counter.

She and Hank sat in one of the booths that lined the perimeter of the diner. A tabletop jukebox sat on each lime-green table and the booths were the same bright red as the lunch counter stools.

They'd each driven over separately from the clinic and now she watched him pick up his fork to dig into his second slice of peach pie.

"I can't let you help me find my stalker for free," she told him, wrapping her hands around her coffee cup. "This may take a while and you've got your vet clinic to run and your own life to live."

He cut off a huge chunk of pie with his fork. "Actually, I'm on vacation so I have all the time in the world."

"And you want to spend it with me?"

He looked up at her, his pie-laden fork poised in the air. "Why not? One of my brothers is a cop and another is a bounty hunter, so maybe catching criminals is in my blood."

"But they get paid for their work."

"And I'm a veterinarian, not a bounty hunter. So unless you want me to neuter your stalker when we catch him, you don't need to pay me."

Rachel watched him eat the rest of his pie, wondering why he'd volunteer to help her catch a stalker, especially since they'd only met this morning. She worried that he might have ulterior motives. "Hank, if you won't take my money, then at least let me help you."

"Help me?" His brow furrowed. "I thought we already cleared up that misunderstanding this morning. I don't have any problems, especially in *that* area."

She suppressed a smile. "No, I'm talking about the secret you revealed to the group tonight—that you've never been in love."

He shrugged. "Well, it's true, but I don't consider that a problem. I just wanted to contribute something to the conversation."

Rachel didn't believe him, although she suspected *he* believed it. In her profession, people often said things, even as jokes, that touched on a real issue in their life. "You're thirty-five years old and have never fallen in love? You don't find that...unusual?"

He considered the question. "I've had a busy life, first looking out for my little brothers, then college, vet school, and starting my business. Now I'm at a point where I can finally start having some fun."

"And a different woman every weekend is fun?"

He grinned. "I think most single men would agree with me that it's the definition of fun. And how about you, Dr. Grant? I believe you mentioned some-thing at my appointment about a *raft of blind dates*." He chuckled, using his fork to scrape up the last remnants of pie. "Sounds like I'm not the only one playing the field."

"I'm officially off the field," Rachel informed him. "Just so we're clear."

"Got it." Then he pulled a quarter from the pocket and of his blue jeans and started scrolling through the song titles on the mini jukebox. "Any requests?"

"I like classical music. How about you?"

"Classic rock. So that's one sign that we're not a match, even if you weren't off the field." He kept scrolling. "But I'm still going to help you catch your stalker, even if I have to kiss you over and over again."

Feeling another telltale blush crawl up her cheeks, Rachel quickly went on the offensive. "And I'm going to figure out why you can't fall in love, even if I have to ask you questions over and over again."

Aware that he was about to protest, she plucked the quarter from his fingers and dropped it into the coin slot on the tabletop jukebox. Then she pressed B2 on the button panel.

Hank's blue eyes widened in surprise as the music began to play. "Is that the tune to 'Don't Stop Believin'' by Journey?"

"Yes, played by a string quartet. It's one of my favorites."

"Mine too." He laughed. "I never thought I'd be a fan of classical music, but this isn't bad."

"And it's a sign we can find common ground, so at least give me a chance to dig into that big brain of yours. Unless you're afraid..." She let the words linger in the air, intently watching his face.

"Afraid?" His steely blue gaze locked with hers. "Not a chance."

"Good," she said, hiding her smile as she pulled a notepad and pen from her purse. "Then let's get started."

5

Hank sat crouched low in the front seat of his black pickup truck. He'd parked it across the street and half a block down from Rachel's house.

It was almost one o'clock in the morning, but he didn't plan to go anywhere until he was sure she was safe. For all he knew, her stalker could be watching her from another parked car on the street or skulking in the bushes near her house.

Reaching for the can of soda on his console, he took a deep swig, hoping the caffeine would help keep him awake.

His head still hurt from that collision with the bull, although the pain was more of a heavy, dull ache now instead of a buzzsaw in his brain.

He'd expected Rachel to use a buzzsaw to dig into his innermost secrets, but instead of interrogating him at the diner, she'd talked more about her own life and asked him about his.

Now Hank realized how much he'd revealed to her over that third slice of peach pie. She knew about his childhood and the death of his parents—and way too much about his love life.

Which made finding her stalker even more urgent, because he didn't like sharing his feelings. He didn't see any point to it.

Feelings didn't pay the bills or fix fences or solve problems. He was a man of action, which was why he'd kissed Rachel when she'd given him the opportunity.

And it made him feel amazing.

Kissing her was even better than he'd imagined, and he'd been imagining it from almost the moment they'd met. But he didn't plan to ever share that with her. Rachel had made it very clear she had no romantic interest in him.

Although the way she'd kissed him back made him wonder. "No," he told himself aloud. "Don't go there, Holden."

The last thing he wanted to do was bungle this job because Rachel got in his head. That's what feelings did to a man—they made him weak and impulsive.

The best way to protect her was to ignore these feelings stirring inside him and concentrate on the

63

job at hand. Reaching into his shirt pocket, he pulled out the list she'd made right before they'd left the diner.

The list contained the names of men she had interacted with in the past few months—especially the ones she'd had a conflict with or any type of unusual interaction, negative or positive.

Rachel hadn't included any names of her male patients due to confidentiality issues. But she'd already ruled them out with the handwriting comparisons.

The first one on her list was her next door neighbor, Newt Beaufort. Apparently, he had his eye on her lot, hoping to buy her out so he could build on both lots. Hank wasn't sure how stalking would help his cause.

Then he focused on the fifteen blind dates on the list. According to her, she'd never gone out more than once or twice with any of them. But a few hadn't taken her rejection well.

He picked a pencil from his console and circled those names, deciding to check them out first. Maybe his brother Nick could run their names to see if any of them had been in trouble with the law before.

That made him wonder if stalkers were repeat offenders or if they just focused on one victim.

Maybe he'd ask Rachel since she seemed to be the expert in the human mind. He'd been impressed with some of her advice to the Lonely Hearts group, although he didn't agree with all of it. Seemed to him like people wasted a lot of time trying to understand their feelings.

Bright headlights suddenly flashed on his front windshield, making him wince. He slid down even further in the seat, trying to fold his large body into the small space between the door and the console.

Peering through the lower half of the driver's side window, he saw the car pass Rachel's house and continue down the block.

It was an old red Buick, not a Taurus, and most likely not the stalker. He sat up higher and watched the car's progress in the rearview mirror. It made a right turn at the corner of the block and disappeared.

False alarm.

A dog barked in the distance and he thought of Georgie waiting for him at home. She was used to him leaving at all hours to attend to difficult births or other animal emergencies.

He knew he'd find her sleeping comfortably on the sofa when he returned home, snuggled under her favorite blanket. He reclined against the car seat once more, his gaze moving to Rachel's home.

She lived in a modest craftsman-style house constructed of wood and stone. A white porch swing hung from a white wooden beam on the covered front porch and red rose bushes twined around the white fence posts.

She had reluctantly agreed to let him follow her home so he could be sure she got safely inside her house. He'd almost suggested another kiss at her door, just in case the stalker was watching, but he didn't want to push his luck.

Then, instead of heading home like he'd planned, Hank found himself circling the block and parking across the street to keep watch.

Maybe it his sense of duty. Or the fact that he didn't have anywhere else he needed to be. Rachel needed him, whether she liked it or not. At least until they tracked down her stalker. Because he wasn't about to let anything happen to her on his watch.

Headlights illuminated the cab of his pickup once more, only this time they were coming from the opposite direction. He hunched down, not wanting to draw the attention of neighbors who might question a stranger parked on their block in the middle of the night.

He watched the car through the rearview mirror, realizing as it drove past him that it was the same red Buick he'd seen before. Grabbing his pen, he quickly jotted down the license plate number. It was too dark to get a good look at the driver, but he was almost certain it was a man.

It took all his willpower to wait for the Buick to

turn the corner and disappear before he switched on the ignition of his truck and shifted into drive. He hadn't wanted to spook the Buick's driver with the flash of headlights behind him.

In Hank's mind, there was no good reason for a car to drive past Rachel's house twice at this time of night—especially from two different directions. He wanted nothing more than to run the driver down, yank him out of the car, and shove his fist down the man's throat.

But first he needed to be certain he had the right guy. So he held back, not wanting to spook the driver into a high speed chase. After turning the corner out of Rachel's neighborhood, he caught sight of the tail end of the Buick making a left onto the main thoroughfare.

Hank made a left too, then followed at a distance, staying just close enough to keep the Buick in sight. He pictured himself showing up on Rachel's doorstep tomorrow morning with the news that her stalker had been caught.

She'd flash that dazzling smile and throw herself into his arms. He knew too well how perfectly her body fit against his and the way her kiss had almost undone him.

"Get a grip, Holden," he said aloud. This was no time to indulge in fantasies. And imagining that kind of reaction from Rachel was definitely a fantasy. Once her stalker was caught, he'd probably never see her again, unless she insisted on another deep dive into his psyche.

The driver of the Buick maintained a steady speed, apparently unaware or unconcerned that Hank was following him. As they approached the intersection, the light turned yellow and the Buick came to a stop. Hank pulled up behind him just as the light turned red. Then the Buick's tires squealed as it sped into the intersection, just barely missing the cars crossing in the opposite directions.

Hank muttered an oath and hit the steering wheel with the heel of his hand. There were too many cars in the way for him to give chase and the Buick was well out of sight before the stoplight turned green again.

"You'd better run and hide," he muttered, opening his hand to look at the license plate number he'd written on his palm. "Because I'm coming after you."

The next morning, Hank walked into the Pine City Police Station and went in search of his brother, Nick, who worked as a detective on the force. The station was housed in a two-story brick building in the historic district of Pine City, and had served as police headquarters since the nineteenth century. Old horse stables located behind the station had been converted into a community center for neighborhood kids. Hank had even coached a youth basketball team there last year.

As he walked toward Nick's office, a middle-aged K-9 officer waved to him from his desk. "Hey, Hank, how's it going?"

"Good. How about you, Ron? Any more problems with Bruno's scratching?" he asked, referring to the German shepherd the officer worked with on the K-9 unit.

"No, that medication you prescribed cleared it right up."

"Glad to hear it." Hank continued down the hallway, but when he reached Nick's office, the door was locked and his brother was nowhere in sight. Cops bustled around him, a few nodding in recognition as they passed by.

Frustrated and exhausted from his all-night vigil watching Rachel's house, Hank grabbed the nearest empty chair in the hallway and sat down. As a country vet, he was used to working all hours of the day and night, but he'd been feeling a little off since Saturday when that bull had kicked him in the head.

"Man up," he muttered, pulling his cell phone out of his pocket. He typed a text to Nick: *Where are you?*

Hank hit the send button, then followed with a text to Charlie asking if he needed any help at the vet

69

clinic. His third text went to his grandmother, asking her to stop by his place this morning and check on Georgie, because he wasn't sure when he'd be home.

Then he typed out a text to Rachel: *Everything okay?*

Not even a minute passed before she replied: *Everything's good. I'm at work. See you tonight?*

Hank typed out: *Yes.* Then he hit send. They had plans to go out for dinner at Rawlings Steak House, one of Pine City's most popular restaurants. He wasn't sure how busy it would be on a Tuesday night, but he'd be on the lookout for a red Buick in the parking lot.

Realizing he hadn't told Rachel about the Buick yet, he started to text another message to her, then changed his mind. Better to tell her about the red Buick fiasco in person, when he could explain what happened. He still couldn't believe he'd let the driver get away.

Hearing the sound of cowboy boots on the floor, Hank looked up to see Luke Rafferty moving toward him.

"Hey, Hank, what are you doing here?"

Luke was Nick's partner on the force and always looked like he'd just rolled out of bed. His gray suit was as rumpled as his shaggy brown hair.

"I'm waiting for Nick," Hank said, rising to his feet. "Have you seen him?"

"Not for a few days." Luke switched his coffee cup to his left hand, then dug a key out of his right pants pocket, along with several pieces of lint. "Nick's out on an undercover assignment this week." Luke unlocked the door and opened it. "But come on in, maybe I can help you."

"I hope so." Hank followed him into the office. One side looked like it had been hit by a tornado, with folders scattered across the desk, two books lying open on the floor, and papers scattered everywhere.

The other side looked as tidy as Grandma Hattie's chicken coop and he found himself wondering if she'd stopped by to organize Nick's side of the office.

"I wouldn't put it past her," he mused under his breath.

"What's that?"

Hank smiled. "Nothing." Then he handed him a piece of paper with the red Buick's license number on it. "I need someone to run a plate check for me."

"Interesting." Luke took the paper from him, then pushed some file boxes aside on his desk to make room for his coffee cup. "Why does a country vet need a plate check?"

Hank gave him the short version about the stalker situation without revealing his role in it. "I saw this car driving past Dr. Grant's house twice late last night. When I followed him, he sped through a red light and disappeared."

Luke stared at him for a long moment. Then face broke into a wide grin. "You're doing that Cowboy Confidential thing for Miss Hattie, aren't you?"

"How do you know about that?"

"Because that's how Nick snagged Lucy." Luke laughed. "Or maybe it was the other way around. All I know is that he's a man in love and it's pretty disgusting."

"Lucy's great," Hank said, remembering her quirky Christmas gifts. "Did you hear she's going to be my sister-in-law?"

"Sure did. Nick and I even went ring shopping together." Luke shivered as he picked up his coffee cup. "That was an experience I'll never forget."

Hank could just imagine. He liked Rafferty and understood his aversion to marriage and commitment, because he shared it as well. Hopefully, Nick and Lucy would fulfill Grandma's Hattie's wish for great-grandchildren, because Hank couldn't see himself giving up his freedom anytime soon.

"Can you describe the driver of this car?" Luke sat down at his desk and opened his laptop computer. "Approximate age? Hair color? Beard? Anything?"

"No, it was too dark to see a face. All I got was the plate number. I hope it can lead me to her deranged stalker."

Luke typed the plate number into his computer, then looked up at Hank. "How do you know he's deranged?"

"He'd have to be, right? Mailing her creepy love quotes and getting close enough to slip one of them into her coat pocket."

Luke shrugged. "People do crazy things when they're in love—or think they are. But you're right, stalking takes it to a dangerous level. It's usually more about control than affection."

"Rachel said the same thing, but I'll stick with deranged."

Luke grinned. "Rachel, is it?" Then he turned back, quickly typing on his computer. "Dr. Rachel Grant." He whistled low. "Wow, I love redheads."

Hank leaned over to look at the screen and saw the Craig Clinic's website open to Rachel's professional photo and biography. Then he punched Luke's arm. "I thought you were looking up the plate number."

"Oh, right," Luke said, laughing as he closed the website and started typing.

Hank watched him work, relieved that Rafferty hadn't questioned him any further about Cowboy Confidential. The more people who knew about it, the greater the chance that Rachel might find out he'd been hired to protect her. Then she'd know he'd been lying to her from the moment they'd met.

"I've got it," Luke announced as the printer on his desk whirred into action. He handed the sheet of paper to Hank while it was still warm.

"Thanks," he said, reading the name at the top of the page. "Lee Demby."

"If you catch Dr. Grant's stalker, give me a call before you confront the guy," Luke said. "I don't want to have to charge you with assault and battery. Just bring him in and we'll try to make some charges stick."

Hank frowned. "Try? Does that mean he could get away with it?"

Luke sighed. "The stalking laws have gotten tougher, but they can still be difficult to prove and prosecute. Sometimes our hands are tied if there's not a specific law broken."

That's not what Hank wanted to hear, but he'd deal with that possibility later. Right now, he needed to mete out some Holden-style justice.

Later that day, Gina lay stretched across the gray carpet in Rachel's office, her hands clasped behind her head as she stared up at the white tile ceiling. "So if I murdered Kurt, you don't think I could get away with a temporary insanity plea?"

"No." Rachel sat working at her desk. She'd

cleared the entire afternoon to catch up on paper-work and eat lunch with Gina. "And I wouldn't testify for you, if that's your next question."

She closed the file in front of her and placed it on top of a small stack of folders. "I think you should stop fantasizing about ways to kill Kurt. It's not healthy."

"Maybe not, but it's fun. And it makes me feel better." Gina looked over at her. "Don't tell me you never had revenge fantasies about Russell when he left you."

"No, not really." Rachel let her mind wander back to that time in her life. "I cried a lot, from the shock as much as anything. I'd thought we'd been so compatible. He fit the profile of the perfect man: well-educated, a good conversationalist, passionate about his work..."

"And a know-it-all." Gina rolled over onto her stomach and propped herself up on her elbows. "I'm sorry, Rachel, but he was *not* the right man for you. We all knew it."

"What?" Rachel shoved the file aside. "You all thought Russell was wrong for me? Why in the world didn't you tell me?"

"I'm sorry." Gina sat up on her knees. "But we knew you were in love with him. We didn't want you breaking up with Russell based on our opinion—or worse, *not* break up with him and then our friendship falls apart because you know how we feel about him."

"I still wish you would have said something." Rachel tried to hide her disappointment, wondering what else her friends were keeping from her. "I'll admit that after he left me, I had mixed feelings. I was so hurt—and felt so abandoned—but at the same time, a small part of me wondered if I ever really knew him."

Gina sighed. "You're better off without him, Rach."

"And maybe you're better off without Kurt." She pushed back her chair and stood up. "Maybe if you spent less time seeking revenge and more time focused on what you want your future to look like, you'd be happier." She held up one finger. "And as a bonus, you wouldn't be sent to prison for murder."

"Ooh, that gives me an idea." Gina stood up and approached the desk. "We could switch murders! Like in that Alfred Hitchcock movie, *Strangers on a Train*. You can kill Kurt while *I* have an alibi. And then I'll fly to Africa and hunt down Russell while *you* have an alibi." Her face brightened. "I think I even have enough frequent flyer points for the trip."

"The only trip you might be going on is a seventy-two-hour psych hold if you keep talking like this." Rachel closed the file she'd been reading and set it aside. "But seriously, Gina, if you think you'd like to talk to a professional, I can recommend any of my colleagues at the clinic. I believe Dr. Craig has openings in his schedule."

"Ooh, is he the married therapist or the cute one who looks like sexy, young Sigmund Freud?"

Rachel laughed. "The married one. Sorry, but Sigmund, otherwise known as Noah Lopez, only works at the clinic part time. And Jenna Rifkin, the other therapist in our group, goes on maternity leave in another month. So I think Dr. Craig would be the best fit for you."

"Can't you just be my therapist?"

Rachel shook her head. "As your friend, I can't be objective. That wouldn't be fair to you."

"But you're my therapist in the Lonely Hearts group."

"That's more of a support group that I moderate," she explained. "Although I admit the line is a little fuzzy. But since it's the only group of its kind in Pine City, I didn't want to exclude you from it."

"I am kind of a mess," Gina admitted. "Or maybe I'm just hungry."

Rachel glanced at the wall clock. "Steven should be here with our lunch soon, although he's picking up food for my partners too, so it might take him a little longer."

"Are you all still happy with your new business partners?"

"It's been great so far. The Craig Clinic has had a wonderful reputation for the past thirty years, so I'm thrilled Dr. Craig was open to taking on partners. All three of us partnered with Dr. Craig at the same time, so I feel like we're on an equal footing. We share overhead expenses and staff. We've got Steven working at reception and our billing clerk works from her home."

"It sounds like a nice setup."

As if on cue, Steven tapped on the door, then walked inside her office carrying a pizza box and a large white bag. He looked younger than his twenty-five years, with short blond hair, green eyes and lots of freckles.

"I've got one pizza, half pepperoni and half veggie," Steven announced. "And one large order of hot wings with extra sauce."

"That sounds perfect," Rachel said, her stomach rumbling. "Thank you, Steven,"

She'd overslept this morning and missed breakfast after staying out late with Hank. Rachel still couldn't quite believe they were going to work together to find her stalker. Or did pretending to be in love qualify as work?

"Oh, that reminds me, Dr. Grant," Steven said as he set the food on a small children's table that she used for play therapy. "You're wanted in Dr. Craig's office for a quick meeting."

She looked longingly at the food. "Right now?"

"Yeah, sorry, I don't know what it's about."

Rachel grabbed a plate and slice of pizza to take with her. "Sorry, Gina. I'll try to hurry back."

"Take your time," Gina called after her. "I have more murders to research."

Certain that would keep her friend busy for a while, Rachel headed to Dr. Craig's office. Along the way her cell phone vibrated, indicating a call. When she saw it was Hank calling, she let it go to voicemail, then walked into Dr. Craig's office.

The other two therapists working at the Craig Clinic, Noah Lopez and Jenna Rifkin, were already seated with Dr. Craig at the small conference table in the center of the room. Dr. Craig's office was the largest in the clinic and had a wall of books on one side, including a popular psychology book he'd written twenty years ago.

"Glad you could join us, Rachel," Jenna said with one hand resting on her swollen belly. "We've got a problem."

"Hope you don't mind that I brought my lunch with me."

Dr. Craig smiled up at her. "Not at all."

Rachel sat down at the table, taking a chair next to Noah. *He did look like a sexy, young Sigmund Freud*, she thought to herself. Now that she had that image in her mind, she couldn't shake it. Noah had asked her out when they'd first joined the clinic together, but she'd turned him down, aware that it wasn't smart to mix business with romance.

He was certainly nothing like Hank. Then her mind drifted to that kiss last night and...

"Rachel?"

Dr. Craig's voice brought her back to the present.

"Oh, I'm sorry. What did you say?"

"I asked how you're doing. We're all very worried about you."

She looked around the table, noting that Noah and Jenna looked more irritated than worried. "I'm fine. What's going on?"

Dr. Craig cleared his throat. "I've asked all of you here because we have some decisions to make. I received a call earlier from a man named Hank Holden. I believe he's a friend of yours?"

"Yes, sort of." There was no way she was going to explain that Hank had started out as her patient, then tackled another patient in her office, and was now pretending to be her boyfriend. "What did he want?"

"Well, he told me that we needed to invest in a security system for your safety." Dr. Craig folded his hands on the table. "He even took the liberty of contacting a security company to pay us a visit this afternoon and recommends not only security cameras and alarms, but also a guard at the door."

She took a bite of her pizza to keep from screaming in frustration. How dare Hank intrude on her professional relationship with her business partners before checking with her?

Maybe she'd overdone it with the personal questions last night and he was in a hurry to catch her stalker and never see her again. She'd learned that he'd lost his parents when he was only eleven and then had taken on the responsibilities of an adult, despite his loving grandparents trying to give him the best childhood they could, considering the circumstance.

"Wait a minute," Noah said. "I thought you were getting a few letters. What changed?"

After another bite of pizza, Rachel told them about the note in her pocket and the concern that her stalker might be escalating. "But I don't want that to impact the clinic. This is a personal issue and Hank never should have contacted you about it."

"I disagree," Dr. Craig said. "We're partners and that means we look out for each other. I don't see anything wrong with investing in some security equipment. It can help keep all of us safe."

"But can we afford it?" Noah asked. "We just started our partnership a few months ago and our budget is so tight." He looked over at Rachel. "It's not that I don't care about what you're going through, but there are confidentiality issues too."

Jenna nodded. "I have to agree with Noah. I have patients who may be intimidated by security cameras or worried that their visits won't be confidential."

Rachel chewed thoughtfully on her pizza, irritated with Hank for starting this mess. She'd laid out a simple plan for him to follow, but he obviously wanted to take the lead. "Let's just forget that Hank Holden ever called here," she said at last. "He overstepped and I feel perfectly safe here."

"Are you sure?" Jenna asked, rubbing her belly. "Stalkers, as we all know, can be unpredictable. Anyone would be scared."

"I'm actually more frustrated than scared," Rachel explained. "I don't know who the stalker is yet or why he's targeting me. But I won't let him dictate my life. Then he really would have power over me."

"Okay, I guess the decision is made." Dr. Craig sighed. "But will you let us know if you change your mind?"

"Yes, of course." She rose from her chair. "And I do appreciate your concern."

He smiled. "That's what partners are for."

Rachel walked out of Dr. Craig's office ready to confront Hank. But before she reached her office, her cell phone buzzed again and Hank's name appeared on the screen. She moved to a secluded alcove in the lobby to answer it. "I can't believe your nerve."

"This Rachel?" demanded a woman's voice with a heavy Texas drawl.

"Yes," she said in surprise. "Who's this?"

"The name's Demby and I'm at 244 Dover Road. I don't have time for anymore nonsense, so come get your man before I shoot him. I'm not gonna tell you twice."

Then the connection was lost.

❧ 6 ❧

Perching on the rough wood floor of the small cabin, Hank watched the older woman across from him. She sat in a rocking chair, her narrow gaze fixed on him and a 22-gauge shotgun in her weathered hands.

"There's been a big mistake," he began.

"I told you to hush." She scowled at him, slowly rocking the chair. Her wispy white hair hung in a loose braid down her back and she wore a blue plaid flannel shirt and a pair of blue denim overalls, along with a pair of sturdy work boots. He couldn't tell if she was sixty or eighty, but the fire in her gray eyes and the way she handled that shotgun told him that she was no pushover.

He leaned his head back against the wall and

stared up at the wooden beams on the ceiling, wondering where he'd gone wrong.

Maybe it was heading straight for Dover Road after Luke had given him the name and address for Lee Demby. Or when he jumped out of his pickup truck and marched toward the front door of the cabin before he'd even made a plan.

Or had it been when he pounded on the cabin door and demanded Demby come out and face him? No, his biggest error had been walking inside the cabin when he realized the door was unlocked. That's when he'd felt the wrong end of a shotgun pushed into his back. Then the woman introduced herself as Mrs. Demby and he quickly learned she did not appreciate trespassers on her property. That's when she made a citizen's arrest.

He called it kidnapping.

The woman hadn't listened to reason when he'd tried to explain, and she refused to tell him where he could find Lee Demby. Hank figured the guy had to be her husband or son. But the real indignity happened when she demanded Hank hand over his cell phone. Given the shotgun pointed at him, Hank had no choice but to comply.

Then he watched her contact the last number he'd dialed on his phone. Now Rachel was on her way here and had no clue what awaited her.

Hank closed his eyes, his head pounding like he'd

been hit by a sledgehammer and there was an odd ringing in his ears. Maybe because he was sleep deprived and hadn't made time to stop for food or coffee since he'd driven away from his stakeout spot on Rachel's street this morning.

Rachel.

That's where it had all gone wrong. He'd agreed to take on this Cowboy Confidential job when he wasn't of sound mind. And now he was paying the consequences.

He could be living his life right now, working as vet by day and looking for fun by night. But instead he'd agreed to take on Rachel and her stalker.

"What the heck's wrong with you?" Mrs. Demby asked, her eyes wide. "You don't look so good."

"I'm allergic to people holding me at gunpoint."

"Oh, so you're a wise guy. I don't care much for wise guys."

A tiger-striped cat sauntered toward him, stopping just long enough to sniff the toe of his cowboy boot before moving on. "Nice-looking cat," he said, hoping to ease the tension between them. "What's his name?"

"That's none of your business."

"Well, actually I'm a veterinarian. Dr. Hank Holden—maybe you've heard of me? I have a clinic with Dr. Dennison out near Route 29."

"Nope." She slowly rocked in her chair, cradling the shotgun like a baby.

He didn't feel well enough to turn on his charm. Usually women of all ages loved him. "Well, I'd be happy to give your cat a checkup if you'd just put down that gun and..."

"You can't fool me, you're no vet," she said bluntly. "They're smart and polite. And they sure wouldn't be foolish enough to try to break my door down. I bet you were planning to rob me."

"I wasn't trying to break your door down or rob you," he protested. "I just came here looking for Lee Demby."

"I know who you're looking for." She leaned forward in the rocking chair. "Heck, everybody in a two-mile radius probably knows, given the way you were carrying on. So maybe you're not a vet or a thief. Maybe you're just plum crazy."

"Then it's a good thing you called a psychologist," he said dryly.

The next twenty minutes passed in silence between them. Finally, Hank heard the sound of tires crunching on gravel.

"Don't move," Mrs. Demby said, rising out of the rocking chair and moving to a window. She pulled back a pink gingham curtain. "Your gal's here and she's a looker, I'll give her that."

"I know." If only the last call on his cell phone had

been to Charlie instead of Rachel. Hank had come out here to play the hero and capture her stalker. Now she'd see him as a wimp who had to be rescued. "You can shoot me now."

"Don't tempt me, boy."

She moved toward the cabin door and opened it just as Rachel reached the front stoop. "Bout time you got here."

Hank watched Rachel's gaze move from Mrs. Demby and the shotgun in her hand to Hank seated on the floor of the cabin next to an old butter churn.

His humiliation was now complete.

"I'm Dr. Rachel Grant," she said to the older woman. "What's going on here?"

"She thinks I wanted rob her," Hank called out.

"Is she right?" Rachel asked, glaring at him in a way that made Hank wonder if she was more dangerous than Mrs. Demby.

"Of course not," he replied. "I came here for you."

"For me?" Rachel marched into the cabin, right past Mrs. Demby and her shotgun. "I think you've done quite enough for me, Hank Holden. You called my clinic director and made a fuss about security alarms and cameras and even a guard? I can't believe your nerve!"

He got up on his feet, wincing after sitting on the hard floor for so long. "Now, hold on just a minute, Rachel..."

Mrs. Demby gave him a warning glance. "Watch yourself, son. This one's got a temper."

"I do," Rachel acknowledged, "but only when I'm at the end of my rope. Can one of you tell me why I'm even here? Because I have no idea."

Hank cleared his throat, ready to take control again. "I'm looking for a man named Lee Demby and got this address from his license plate number."

"Is that what veterinarians do?" Mrs. Demby asked with a skeptical sneer. "Look up folks' license plate numbers?"

"He actually is a vet," Rachel told her, then her gaze narrowed on him. "But go on, Hank. I'd love to hear more."

He took a cautious step toward Mrs. Demby, aware this was probably a sensitive issue for her. "I saw Lee driving an old red Buick by Rachel's house twice, very late last night. When I started to follow him, he blew through a red light and disappeared."

"And I'm just now hearing about this?" Rachel cried. She turned toward Mrs. Demby. "May I borrow your shotgun?"

Hank raised both hands in the air. "Hold on, I'm on your side, Rachel. I thought you'd be happy that I found your stalker."

"Happy?" She took a step closer to him. "Happy that you saw this suspicious red Buick by my house last night and didn't tell me. And apparently, you also were staked out there during the night." She placed her hands on her hips. "What else don't I know?"

Hank considered the question, but knew this wasn't the time or the place to reveal that he'd been secretly hired to protect her. He didn't even want to imagine how she'd react to that piece of information.

At a loss for words, he watched Mrs. Demby retreat to her rocking chair with an odd smile on her face. Then he turned back to Rachel. "Look, maybe I didn't handle it well. I've never gone hunting for a stalker before."

"It's not as fun as it sounds," Mrs. Demby called from her rocker. "Take it from me."

Angry sparks flashed in Rachel's green eyes and a pink flush stained her cheeks. It was an interesting contrast from the cool and collected therapist he'd first met. Something about that dichotomy enticed him.

"I was just doing my job..."

"I never asked you to hunt down my stalker by yourself. We're supposed to be a team and work together. We have a plan, remember? To pretend like we're lovers to draw him out."

Mrs. Demby snorted with derisive laughter.

He looked between the two women and knew he was definitely outnumbered. But now wasn't the time to back down. Not when they were this close to catching her stalker.

Turning to Mrs. Demby, he said, "I know this isn't easy, but you need to tell us where we can find Lee. I'm sure you don't want him to get in trouble for stalking Rachel. If he surrenders peacefully, maybe he can avoid jail and just submit to therapy."

Mrs. Demby stared up at him for a long moment. Then she chuckled. "This is the best time I've had in a good, long while." She stood up and set her shotgun aside. "You've gone to so much trouble to find Lee." She sighed as she moved toward him. "I guess, as much as it pains me, that I'll help you out."

"Thank you," he said with a sigh of relief.

She held out one hand. "I'm Lee Demby. Nice to meet you, Dr. Holden."

Hank froze. "What?"

She pulled her hand back, shaking with laughter. "You caught me fair and square. And I do own a red Buick, but someone stole it out of my yard two weeks ago and I haven't seen it since." She glanced over at Rachel. "I thought Hank here might be the thief, coming back for more."

A satisfied smiled curved Rachel's mouth. "Oh, this is too good."

Hank didn't find it funny at all. He'd just wasted half his day sitting on a cabin floor and staring down a shotgun. "Did you report the car theft to the police?"

"Nah, I like to handle my own business," Lee said.

"And that old junker is mostly held together with baling wire anyway." Then she pointed at him. "But since you're here, you might as well take a look at my mule. Sassy's been terribly gassy lately and I've been meaning to call for a vet."

"I wish I had time to examine Sassy," Hank said, trying to extricate himself from the situation. "But Rachel and I need to talk and..."

"No, go ahead, Hank," Rachel interjected, moving toward the cabin door. "I'll be just fine without you."

Rachel stood in her shower and tipped her head back, letting the hot water wash away the apple-scented shampoo in her hair. Steam filled the bathroom and soft, classical music played on the waterproof speaker that sat on the far corner of the tub.

Molly was dropping by soon to borrow a book, but Rachel lingered in the shower, thinking about her crazy day and wondering if Hank was still stuck at Lee's place looking after her mule. The possibility made her smile. That was the least he deserved after keeping her in the dark about the red Buick and his nighttime vigil outside her home.

What bothered her the most was that she'd noticed a red Buick behind her for most of her drive to the cabin. She'd thought nothing of it at the time, other than it was odd the driver never passed her.

So when Hank mentioned the Buick, she realized it could have very well been her stalker and she'd missed the opportunity to get a good look at the driver.

Tensing at the memory, she lowered her head to let the pulsating spray massage her tense neck and shoulders. Her well-planned day at the office had gone awry from the moment she'd been called into Dr. Craig's office.

Then she thought of Hank, sitting on that cabin floor like a naughty kid sent to the corner. Maybe she'd been too hard on him, Rachel thought to herself as she turned off the water and then opened the shower door to grab a towel, but he needed to realize they were a team.

The doorbell rang just as she put on her white terry cloth bathrobe, her hair hanging in damp ringlets just past her shoulders. She hurried out of the bathroom and down the hallway, making it to the door just as the doorbell rang a second time.

Peering through the peephole, she was surprised to see Hank standing outside, looking a little rumpled from his ordeal at the cabin, but as handsome as ever.

"Rachel?" he called out. "Are you okay?"

"Yes, I'm fine," she said through the door. "What do you want?"

"I've brought you something. A peace offering."

Despite Rachel's irritation with him, her curiosity got the best of her. She undid the locks and then opened the door.

Hank's eyes widened in surprise when he saw her. "Uh...Hello."

"Hello." She cinched her bathrobe tighter, all too aware of his gaze moving slowly over her. "So what did you bring as a peace offering? And please don't tell me it's Lee's mule."

He chuckled. "No, believe me, that poor mule is the last thing you'd want around the house. Turns out Sassy ate too much lush grass, so I ordered some feed to be delivered to Lee's place to make up for the trouble I caused her."

Her irritation at him melted away. "Well, that was nice of you."

"I'm just glad Lee didn't shoot me." Then he held up one hand. "Wait right here and I'll be back with my peace offering."

Okay," she said, watching him hurry down the porch steps to the driveway where he'd parked his pickup. A moment later, he returned holding a khaki duffel bag and leading a handsome dog with a sleek brown coat.

"Her name is Georgie," Hank said as the dog followed him onto the front porch.

Rachel kneeled down to greet her. "Hello, Georgie, you are gorgeous." She smoothed her hands across the dog's sleek fur and silky long ears. "What kind of dog is she?"

"A German shorthaired pointer, or GSP for short."

Rachel rose to her feet and looked at Hank. "I thought they were the ones with the spots."

"Some of them are," he explained. "There are liver-and-white colored GSPs and solid liver GSPs."

She wrinkled her nose. "Who came up with the word *liver* to describe the color of such a beautiful dog?"

"I have no idea. What word would you use to describe her?"

Rachel shrugged. "Maybe mahogany. Or sorrel."

"We have a lot of sorrel horses at Elk Creek Ranch. Have you ever ridden?"

"No, and I've never had a dog either. My brother had terrible allergies, so we didn't have any pets growing up."

"Then how do you feel about me loaning you Georgie for a while? She's very protective and will bark at any stranger who comes near your house."

"My own furry alarm system?" Rachel looked up at

him, half surprised and half thrilled. "I love it!" Then she suddenly remembered she was standing on her front porch in her bathrobe. And Sam Beaufort stood on his lawn next door staring daggers at her. "Let's go inside."

Hank and Georgie both followed her through the front door. Rachel led them to the living room, where Georgie began to explore every nook and cranny. Hank sat down on one side of her blue sofa and Rachel hurried into her room to put on some clothes.

When she emerged, she saw Hank pulling items out of the duffel bag he'd carried in.

"You're more prepared for Georgie than I thought," Hank commented, nodding toward the back wall of the house. "You even have a doggie door."

"It was already here when I moved in," she said, watching Georgie go out the door, then come right back inside. "To be honest, that's one of the things that sold me on this house. Where did you find such a beautiful dog?"

"From a rescue organization when she was about six months old. GSPs are known for their boundless energy and some people aren't prepared for that, especially in a puppy."

He set down the duffel bag. "But Georgie's well-trained now and that's why I thought it might be a good idea for her to stay with you for a while. She seems to have a sixth sense for danger."

"But won't she miss you?"

"Probably not as much as I'll miss her," he admitted. "She's used to staying with my friends or family when I'm out of town, so I'm sure she'll be fine. As long as you don't mind having her."

"Of course not. I've always wanted a dog, but it would have made my twin brother miserable."

"So you're a twin?"

She smiled. "Yes, Brandon's oldest by two minutes. I really miss him and my parents. Texas is a long way from Philly."

"Do you go back often?"

"Not as often as I'd like. My career keeps me busy and I do love it here."

"But you might be safer there," he countered. "Our goal is to find him as soon as possible. But if we're not able to identify your stalker, you don't always want to be looking over your shoulder, do you?"

"Couldn't he just follow me to Philly?"

Hank shook his head. "Doesn't seem likely, especially if it's someone like your neighbor."

She laughed. "Yes, Newt would be thrilled if I ran back home. Then he'd have my lot all to himself."

"So I take it you're not going to scare easily."

She shook her head. "I've never been the type and I don't intend to start now.

Especially of someone who's too cowardly to sign their name to those notes."

Georgie trotted into the room and promptly wedged herself between Hank and Rachel.

"Looks like this girl wants some attention," Rachel said, laughing.

"I let her have the run of my house, but I can bring her crate inside if you'd like her to sleep in it tonight. She's fine either way."

"She can sleep with me," Rachel told him, still focused on the dog. "Or on the sofa or wherever she wants."

"I brought all her favorite toys, along with dog food, some treats, food and water dishes, and a leash." He picked up a tennis ball from the pile of toys. "Georgie," he said, getting the dog's attention before throwing the ball down the long hallway. "Go get it!"

Georgie scampered off, her toenails clicking on the tile. A moment later, she brought the ball back in her mouth and dropped it at Hank's feet before running full tilt into the kitchen and out the doggie door.

"Well, Georgie seems happy to be here." Hank stood up. "So I guess I'd better get going. Call me if you need anything."

"I'll be fine, especially now that I have my new cute alarm system." She walked him to the front door and out onto the porch. "I've also got good locks on the doors and a can of bear spray hidden in every room."

"You are well prepared." He chuckled as climbed down the porch steps to the sidewalk.

"See you tomorrow."

"Aren't you forgetting something?" Rachel called out to him from the porch.

Hank turned around. "What?"

"We're supposed to be in love, remember? You should at least give me a kiss on the cheek in case he's watching."

Without saying a word, Hank closed the distance between them in three long strides. Before she even knew what was happening, he wrapped his arms around her waist and lifted her until Rachel's face was level with his, her feet dangling in the air.

Then he moved his mouth to kiss her along one cheek in a sensuous, downward path to her mouth. Then his kiss devoured her as he slowly turned in a full circle on the porch, still holding her up in his arms.

Rachel's hands clasped his broad shoulders as she leaned into him, forgetting about Newt or anyone else who might be watching.

When Hank finally broke the kiss, he loosened his embrace just enough for her to slowly slide down the length of him until her feet finally touched the ground. "Do you think he's convinced?" he asked huskily.

She blinked up at him, trying to catch her breath. "I think the entire block is convinced."

Then Hank collapsed at her feet.

7

Slowly, Hank awoke to someone pressing their fingers into his bare chest.

"*Rachel?*" he asked wondering if he was dreaming.

"No," said an unfamiliar voice. "I'm Molly Loomis, a friend of Rachel's."

He opened his eyes to see a woman about Rachel's age wearing a white medical coat over a pair of dark-blue scrubs. She had blond hair pulled into a neat ponytail and was standing over him and gently prodding his chest.

"It's good to see you awake," Molly told him. "I'm an ER doctor at Pine City General Hospital, and I'm just checking to see if you have any cracked ribs."

Cracked ribs?

Confused, Hank tipped up his head from the pillow just far enough to see that his shirt had been unbuttoned and lay open for her examination. Fortunately, he still had on his jeans and boots.

Then his gaze fell on Georgie, who lay atop the teal bedspread, her chin resting on his knee and her big brown eyes looking soulfully at him.

"Where's Rachel?" Hank asked, looking around the room.

"I'm right here." Rachel walked into the bedroom with a glass of water that she set on the antique nightstand. "Are you okay?"

"I don't know. What happened?" The last thing he remembered was leaving her house and walking to his pickup truck.

"You passed out," Rachel told him. "I had to call over a few of the neighbors to help me carry you into the house and put you in my guestroom. Even Newt pitched in, although he complained the whole time."

"Then Rachel called me." Molly pulled out a stethoscope from her black leather bag. "Fortunately, I was already on my way over." After gently placing the earpieces of the stethoscope into her ears, she continued the examination, pressing the cold, round chest-piece near his sternum. "Now, please stop talking for a minute while I listen to your heart and lungs."

Hank obeyed her, looked around the bedroom and noticing the light-gray walls and his cowboy hat atop an antique dresser next to a neat stack of psychology books. The room had a nine-foot ceiling with white crown molding and a ceiling fan whirling in slow circle above him. White lace curtains fluttered as cool evening air drifted in through the cracked window.

"Okay, now can you sit up for me, please," Molly told him, moving with a brisk efficiency as she placed the stethoscope on his upper back. "Take a deep breath."

He followed her commands, certain he was just fine. His head felt a little better than it had in days and the ringing in his ears was gone.

At last, Molly stepped away from the bed and placed the stethoscope in her hands. "Your heart and lungs sound good. Have you had issues with fainting recently?"

"No, I've never fainted before in my life." He looked over at Rachel. "Is that what really happened?"

She walked over next to Molly. "You dropped like a rock. Luckily, I was there to break your fall, so you didn't hit your head or break any bones."

"Well, that's good," he said wryly. "One concussion in a week is enough."

"Hold on," Molly said, scowling. "You suffered a concussion this week?"

"Last Saturday," Hank replied, now wishing he'd kept his mouth shut. "I had a minor collision with a bull. According to Dr. Culbertson, I got a mild concussion and a few cuts and bruises."

"And how have you been feeling since then?" Molly asked.

He shrugged. "Not bad. Headaches off and on. A little dizziness, but that might be due to not getting any sleep last Monday night."

"And almost getting shot this afternoon," Rachel chided. "Why didn't you tell me you were hurt?"

"I'm fine." He looked over Molly. "Back me up, Doc."

"Whoa!" Molly held up both hands. "Almost shot? And pulling all-nighters? Just days after a concussion? No wonder you fainted." She shook her head. "Your body just sent a big signal that you need to take it easy and heal up."

"I wasn't almost shot; I was just held at gunpoint by an old lady in a cabin," Hank said, defending himself. "But we worked that out and I'm fine now."

Molly just stared at him. At last, she said, "You're not fine until I say you're fine. Now I'm going to ask both of you a few questions." She turned to Rachel first. "Have you noticed Hank experiencing any slurred speech?"

"No."

"How about confusion or agitation?"

Rachel hesitated. "Well, he has been agitated a few times, but usually for a good reason."

"Very good reason," Hank muttered, angry at himself for not fainting somewhere more private so he wouldn't have two women fussing over him.

Molly turned to Hank. "Have you experienced any episodes of numbness or weakness?"

"None," he said, sitting up higher in the bed.

"Vomiting or nausea?"

"Nope. In fact, I'm starving." He reached out to pet Georgie's head, just to reassure her that he was fine.

"Well, hunger's always a good sign," Molly acknowledged. She started packing up her medical bag. "In my opinion, you've been pushing yourself too hard, Hank. This fainting spell was your body's way of telling you to slow down."

"Okay," he said, not making any promises.

"That means, for the next two weeks, no alcohol. At least eight hours of sleep every night. And I want you to avoid any activity that might lead to another head injury. Rachel told me you're a country vet, so you really need to be extra cautious around large animals."

"He's on vacation right now," Rachel told her, "so that shouldn't be an issue."

"Perfect." Molly pulled a business card from a pocket of her lab coat and placed it on the nightstand. "Here's my number if you have any questions.

You should also call Dr. Culbertson for a follow-up soon. "

"Got it," Hank said, ready to be alone with Rachel again.

"And you'll keep an eye on him, Rach?" Molly asked her friend. "And call me if you notice any of those symptoms I mentioned or anything else that concerns you."

"I will. In fact, I'll be keeping him here tonight, just to make sure he's okay." Then Rachel turned to him. "And I don't want to hear any arguments about it."

Hank smiled. "No arguments from me."

"Perfect," Molly said. "And Rach, would you mind fixing him something to eat? I just want to observe him for a little while longer to make sure he's okay."

"Of course." Rachel looked over Hank. "What food sounds good to you?"

"Honey buns," he said without hesitation.

Rachel winced. "I'm sorry, but I don't have any honey buns on hand. Anything else?"

"I'm fine with whatever you've got."

She flashed her beautiful smile at Hank as she headed out of the bedroom. "Then I'll make you some of my favorite foods from Philly."

Molly closed the bedroom door behind Rachel, then looked over at Hank. "Get ready for some delicious potato-cheese pierogis."

"That'll be a first for me."

Her kind bedside manner suddenly evaporated as she moved closer to the bed.

"All right, Hank," Molly said, her voice low and intense. "Tell me how you're *really* feeling. Because we hired you to protect Rachel, even though we *hate* keeping this secret from her. But now I'm wondering if you're up to the job."

In a flash, the caring doctor had morphed into a fiercely loyal friend. That made Hank like her even more.

"I'm up to the job," he shot back, not about to let her fire him. "How do you know I didn't fake passing out so I could spend the night here? Rachel's already forbidden me from staking out her house again."

She gave him a sidelong glance. "Did you fake it?"

"You're the doctor," he said, evading the question. "You tell me."

Molly's unflinching gaze studied him for a long moment. "Okay, maybe you are up to the job, even with a concussion. If her ex-fiancé hadn't left her, we wouldn't be as worried, but knowing Rachel's alone with a stalker out there..." Molly closed her eyes for a brief moment, then she continued. "You have to understand, my cousin had a stalker who seemed harmless at first too. Now she's in a wheelchair and he's in prison."

"I won't let anything happen to Rachel," he

promised, keeping his voice low. "I give you my word."

"Okay. I believe you." She glanced over at Georgie, who hadn't moved from Hank's side. "And your gorgeous dog seems to adore you. So you can't be all that bad."

"Gee, thanks."

She smiled, resuming her professional air as she picked up her medical bag. "Do you have any questions for me about your condition before I leave?"

"Not about my condition," he said as the pungent aroma of onions and garlic began to drift through the closed bedroom door. "But tell me everything you know about Rachel's ex-fiancé."

Rachel awoke with a start, her heart pounding as she quickly scanned her dark bedroom. For a moment, she didn't understand what had awakened her. Then she heard the sound of frantic barking outside her window.

Georgie.

Hank had told her Georgie would bark whenever strangers were near the house. If the dog was in the backyard, that might mean her stalker was too. And this would be the perfect chance to catch him.

Throwing back the vintage quilt covering her,

Rachel jumped out of bed, wearing only her blue-and-white pajama pants and a matching blue cropped T-shirt.

She grabbed the can of bear spray from the drawer in her nightstand as the barking continued, then ran to her bedroom door, her bare feet slapping against the hardwood floor.

So many thoughts crowded her sleep-fogged brain as she unlocked the door and pulled it open. *Was someone really out there? Would Georgie's barking wake the neighbors? Should she call the police or was it a false alarm?*

As she made her way down the hall, the guestroom door swung open and Hank barreled out, running full tilt into Rachel. By some of feat of grace and luck, he wrapped his arms around her waist and twisted his body, pulling her tightly against his bare chest so his body became a barricade between her and hallway wall.

His back slammed against the wall with a loud thud, rattling the framed photographs hanging just a few feet away.

"Are you okay?" he asked as she turned to face him.

He stood shirtless and barefoot before her, clad only in blue jeans. She swallowed hard, trying to catch her breath. "Of course. You're the one who's supposed to avoid collisions, not me. Are *you* all right?"

"I'm fine," he replied, his attention already diverted by Georgie's incessant barking. "She's in the backyard. You stay here while I go check it out."

"No way," she said to his back, since he was already halfway down the hall. She quickly caught up with him. "You're the one who should stay here. You're supposed rest, remember?" She held up her can of bear spray. "I've got this covered."

He ignored her as he marched toward the sliding glass doors leading out to the backyard. Georgie's barking had slowed now and she raced over to them when Hank slid open the glass door.

"Hey, girl," he called out, "who's out there?"

As if the dog understood him, Georgie moved toward the chain-link fence on the back side of Rachel's yard, where a narrow dirt alley lay between her property and the neighbor's fence.

She walked over to the fence and looked around, but didn't see anything unusual. Her gaze moved in the direction of Newt's house, where a single light glowed in a window. But otherwise it looked peaceful.

They watched Georgie pace back and forth as she stared into the alley, growling low in her throat.

"I don't see anyone," Rachel whispered, standing close to Hank, her bear spray at the ready.

"I don't either." His bare, thick-muscled arm pressed against hers, but Rachel didn't move away. She felt safe with him in a way that she'd never felt safe before. A mockingbird warbled in the distance, breaking the tension in the air.

Georgie's growl finally ended with a low, unsettled whine, then she moved in front of Hank and sat down.

"Good girl," he told her, gently patting her back and shoulder. Then he looked over at Rachel. "I'm going to walk the neighborhood."

"Then I'm going with you," she said, hoping that might dissuade him. He looked better than he had a few hours ago. His color was back to normal and his eyes were clear. But she didn't want to risk him passing out on her again—especially if they ran into her stalker.

He shook his head. "Rachel, listen..."

"Let's just go inside and turn off the lights. Then we can keep watch in the living room. Maybe we'll see someone out there."

His jaw clenched, but he finally relented. "Okay, I guess we can do that."

Relief washed through her as they headed back into house, locking the sliding glass door once more and putting the security bar back in the track to prevent anyone from opening it from the outside.

"Actually, I have a favor ask you," Hank said as they moved toward the living room.

Rachel didn't turn on any lights as she walked over to the fireplace, using only the glow of her cell phone screen to light her way. "What kind of favor?"

"Do you ever help people with their memories? Because I don't remember what happened before I passed out today and it feels like I'm forgetting something important."

She delayed giving him an answer by busying herself with lighting the fire. The only thing he could be forgetting was their kiss. She'd been reminding herself their romance was fake even during the times it felt real to her. And that kiss on the porch had definitely felt real.

Rachel placed two split logs on the grate, then crumpled a sheet of newspaper between them and added kindling on top before lighting it with a long wooden match. All she knew for certain was that he wanted her help. And after all he'd done for her, the least she could do was give it to him.

Rachel carefully added two more log on the grate as the flames began to consume the kindling, then she rose to her feet. "I think I can help you."

She turned and saw Georgie reclined under the coffee table, busy gnawing on a wishbone-shaped chew toy tucked between her front paws.

Hank stood next to the sofa, looking as big and bold as ever, despite his injuries. His eyes seemed even bluer now as he looked at her, if that was possible, and her heart leaped in her chest. A reaction that surprised her given everything that had happened today.

She'd been annoyed with him. Angry. Frustrated. Worried. And now...tempted.

Hank moved toward her until they stood in the space between the fireplace and the coffee table. "Will you help me?

She nodded. "What's the last thing you remember?"

"Walking to the driveway to head home. Is that where I collapsed?"

"No. I called out to you, and you turned around and came back to the front porch." She could see his brow furrowed in concentration. "Do you remember that?"

"I'm trying, but it's just a blank."

"There's one method we could try..." Her voice trailed off as she weighed the implications. But she wasn't his therapist, she reminded herself, so the feelings stirring inside of weren't an issue of professional ethics.

Hank took another step close to her. "I'm game for anything."

"Okay, then let's do a re-enactment." Flames crackled in the hearth behind her. "We'll do it in here, though, since it's dark outside, if that's all right with you."

He nodded. "Sure, let's get started."

"So I called you back to the front porch because I wanted to keep up the pretense that we're a couple..."

"In case the stalker was watching," he finished for her. "Then what?"

"Then you...picked me up off the ground." She reached for his hands and placed them around her waist.

"Like this?" he asked, lifting her up as if she weighed nothing.

She nodded, her throat suddenly very dry. "Yes, but closer."

He pulled her tight against him, his mouth only a hairbreadth away from hers. "I think it's starting to come back to me," he said, his voice low. He placed a light, tender kiss on her brow. "Like that?"

She set her hands on his shoulders to steady herself. "No."

His lips brushed against her cheek. "Like this?"

"Yes," she repeated, trying to keep her breathing steady. "Sort of like that."

Hank trailed light, sensuous kisses down her cheek, until his lips were only inches from her own.

"I remember," he murmured, right before his mouth caught hers, so perfect and pleasurable she could only fall headfirst into his kiss.

Her hands impatiently spanned his broad shoulders, pulling him closer, silently imploring him to deepen the kiss. To quench the impossible thirst he created inside her. Alarm bells went off in her head, but she ignored them, reveling in his embrace.

She slowly surfaced from the haze of passion enveloping them both. She traced her hands over his bare chest, her fingers trailing up his neck until she cupped his face in her hands. She stroked her thumbs at the corners of his mouth, his skin rough with whiskers.

They broke the kiss gradually, Hank dropping tiny kisses on her cheeks and the tip of her nose. Rachel planting soft, swift kisses on his lips.

"Do you remember now?" she asked him as the fire blazed behind them.

"I'll never forget it again," he said, releasing her the same way he'd done on the porch. Then he took step back. "And this is when I passed out?"

She nodded. "It scared me to death."

"Sorry," he said with a smile. "I'll try not to do that to you again."

Reminded of his injury, she pulled him toward the sofa. "The best way not to scare me is to do exactly what Molly told you, which is to take it easy. Your sleep's already been disturbed, so why don't you rest here while I warm up those leftover pierogis. We can eat them in front of the fire before we go back to bed."

Hank reached out one hand, gently tucking a stray wisp of her hair behind her ear. His tender gesture almost made her change her mind and fall back into his arms.

Instead, she turned and walked out of the room, heading straight into the kitchen. Rachel opened the refrigerator door and just stood there for a long moment, letting the cool air bathe her flushed face.

For a fake boyfriend, he sure knew how to make her feel like their romance was the real thing.

A short time later, they sat together on her sofa, eating the leftover pierogis she'd warmed up in the microwave. The house was completely dark except for the fire crackling in the stone hearth.

"Do you think my stalker was really out there?" she asked him.

Hank leaned his head back against the sofa. "I don't know. I hope not. Georgie has also been known to bark at cats occasionally."

Georgie got up from her resting spot under the coffee table at the sound of her name and stood in front of the sofa.

Rachel reached out to pet her. "You're such a sweet girl. I've been thinking about getting a dog for myself. Maybe a rescue dog like her."

"It's a big commitment," he told her. "It takes a while for any dog to adjust to a new home." He fed Georgie a small piece of a pierogi from the platter on the coffee table. "Just like people have to adjust to change, whether they like it or not."

Maybe it was the intimacy of the dark room or the wistfulness she heard in his voice that compelled her to say, "Like you had to adjust after your parents died?"

A smile played on his lips as he stared at the fireplace. "Sorry, Rachel, but I'm not really in the mood for psychotherapy right now."

"This isn't therapy," she said softly. "It's just talking between friends."

He turned his head, his deep blue eyes staring into hers. "So we're friends now?"

"I hope so."

Hank's gaze moved back to the fire. "Then can I ask you a question?"

"Of course," she said, reaching for the flannel blanket on the back of the sofa and draping it over the lower half of her body.

"Why didn't you add your ex-fiancé to the suspect list you made for me?"

Rachel froze. She hadn't realized Hank knew about Russell. Then she remembered his sudden entrance at the Lonely Hearts group meeting. He must have heard her talking about him. "I didn't add him because he's not even on the same continent as I am."

"How do you know? Have you been in touch with him?

She picked at a piece of fluff on the blanket. "No,

not at all."

"And how do you feel about that?"

She looked over at him, then started laughing. "Okay, now who's playing therapist?"

"You're avoiding the question," he said as Georgie curled herself around his feet.

"The truth is that I don't know how to answer. I think I've convinced myself that I can't move on to another relationship until I figure out what went wrong with Russell." She sighed. "Maybe that's why none of my blind dates have worked out."

"Or they just weren't your type."

Feeling cozy under the warmth of the blanket, she stared into the fire for a long time, thinking about everything that had happened in the past year. "The funny thing is," she said at last, "I'm not sure I'd give that same advice to one of my patients. I'd tell them to learn what they can from the experience and move on. Ruminating over the past just keeps you stuck there. Like a tire spinning in the mud."

She looked up at Hank and saw that he was fast asleep, his head tilted slightly on the sofa cushion. It was the perfect opportunity to look at him for as long as she wanted. She noticed his eyelashes were long and thick and there was small linear scar just above one eyebrow. His hair had a slight curl to it and his jawline was covered with thick dark whiskers.

Moving carefully, she draped half of the blanket

over him, then turned to watch the flames in the hearth.

"Wake me up if he needs me, Georgie," she murmured as her eyes drifted shut.

❧ 8 ❧

The next morning, Rachel awoke to find herself wrapped in Hank's embrace and her head resting on his broad shoulder. His eyes were closed and his even breathing told her he was still asleep.

She fit so perfectly against him that she didn't want to move, but she could see her cell phone on the coffee table and knew the alarm was set to go off any moment.

Moving very slowly, she extricated herself from his arms, instantly missing his warmth. She tucked the flannel blanket around him, then saw Georgie, now awake and alert, sniffing at the empty plate on the coffee table that had contained the pierogis.

"Hang on," she whispered to the dog. "I'll get you some food in a minute."

Rachel grabbed her phone and switched off the

alarm, then a moment later, an unfamiliar number popped onto the screen and her ringtone began to play the upbeat lyrics of "It's a Good Day" by Perry Como.

"Wow," Hank said, stretching his arms and shoulders. "That song is way too peppy this early in the morning. I'd need about three cups of strong black coffee before I could listen to that."

She laughed as she sent the call to voicemail. "Are you always this grumpy in the morning?"

"Yes."

Rising from the sofa, she picked up the blanket and began to fold it. Then her phone rang again, belting out more Perry Como. "Who in the world is calling me this early?"

Hank sat up quickly, instantly alert. "You don't recognize the number?"

"No. And I sent the first one to voicemail." Her finger hovered over the screen. "Should I answer it?"

"Go ahead," he urged. "And put it on speaker."

Taking a deep breath, Rachel tapped the speaker button before answering the call. "Hello?"

"Hello, is this Dr. Rachel Grant?" asked a woman on the other end of the line.

"Yes, it is. May I ask who's calling?"

"This is Midge Berman. You may know my good friend, Edith Cummings. She raves about your Lonely Hearts group."

"Oh," Rachel said, taking a moment to make the connection. *This was Jonathan Kasper's sister-in-law.* She'd never met Midge, but she'd read her daily column and enjoyed the woman's wit. "Yes, Ms. Berman, what can I do for you?"

She saw Hank relax and lean back against the sofa, closing his eyes once more. He was still shirtless and more than a little distracting. Then Rachel realized she'd missed part of the conversation.

"I'm sorry," Rachel interrupted. "What did you say?"

"That you must call me Midge and you absolutely must come on my TV show."

"*Pine City People?*" Rachel asked, certain there must be a mistake. "Why would you want me on the show?"

"Because we highlight the citizens of the best town in Texas. And you're certainly worth highlighting."

Rachel hesitated, thrown completely off guard. "May I ask how you selected me?"

"Actually, my brother-in-law, Jon Kasper, recommended you. He'd been a patient at the Craig Clinic for years for his claustrophobia, but after only a few sessions with you, he's completely cured."

"Well, as I'm sure you know," Rachel began slowly, "I can't discuss who may or may not be a patient of mine. But I'm always happy to hear about people who've overcome obstacles for a happier life."

"Spoken like a true professional," Midge declared. "Now, you'll need to be here by three o'clock this afternoon. That should give you plenty of time in hair and makeup. And..."

"Wait, you're talking about today?"

"Yes, we had a sudden cancellation, but I believe this is perfect timing. Now you can tell the audience about your group's plan to boycott Valentine's Day."

Rachel glanced at Hank, who looked amused by the conversation. "It's not an official boycott; it's just a type of personal coping mechanism."

"Yes, that's exactly what I'd like to talk about."

The last thing Rachel wanted to do was appear on television. "I'm sorry, but today just won't work for me. My schedule is pretty full."

"May I ask what time you have your last appointment?"

"Three o'clock."

"Oh, then that's perfect. Jon told me his appointment is at three and he's very excited to see you on the show, so I'll tell him to cancel."

"What? You can't do that."

"In fact," Marge continued, "he told me that a man actually assaulted him in your office at his last appointment. Of course, he's not usually the litigious type, but if he heard you were uncooperative about being on my show, I'm not sure what he might do..."

Rachel almost dropped the phone at Midge's not-so-subtle extortion attempt. She looked over at Hank, who was holding a contented Georgie in his lap.

"Okay," she agreed, feeling she didn't have much choice. The last thing she wanted to do was tell her clinic partners that they might get sued. "I guess I will be on your show today."

"Wonderful! I'm sure my audience will love you. See you at three o'clock sharp. Bye, dear."

"Bye," Rachel said as the call ended.

"I take it that wasn't your stalker?"

"No," she said briskly. "But I think I've just been blackmailed."

That afternoon, Rachel sat in the green room on the set of *Pine City People*, her hands clenched around each arm of the chair. A charcuterie board of various cheeses and smoked meats sat on a table, along with some fresh cut fruit, but Rachel couldn't eat a bite.

She could not go out there.

It wasn't nerves. *Pine City People* was simply a late-afternoon talk show that featured local citizens, a cooking segment, and an informational piece by the

Jolly Greengrocer on the fruit of the month. She'd presented at enough mental health seminars and conferences to be confident in her speaking abilities.

It wasn't doubts about the interview either. She had a file full of information and studies about holiday depression and ways to alleviate it. Techniques that could really help people. She'd also written a short speech outlining why some people, including members of her Lonely Hearts group, might want to boycott Valentine's Day.

There was only one reason she couldn't go on live television. And that reason was her hair.

Her really big hair.

Justine, the show's hairdresser, had moussed and back-combed and spritzed her thick red hair until it took on a life of its own. At five nine, she'd always been aware of her height, preferring to wear flats so she didn't tower over other people. But her shoes hardly mattered with four inches of hair sticking up on her head. She looked like an Amazon prom queen.

No one would take her seriously with this hair.

A harried assistant stuck his head in the door. "Five minutes to air, Dr. Grant."

"Wait," she cried before he could disappear among all the cameras and cables and chaos. "What's your name?"

"Devon," he said, scanning his clipboard. He was head shorter than Rachel with a wiry build and dark stringy hair. And his head never stopped moving as he evaluated everything around him.

"I can't go out there, Devon."

The young man looked up, his eyes wide behind his thick glasses. "That is *not* an option, Dr. Grant. You have to go on." He checked his watch. "In four minutes and twenty-five seconds."

"I can't go on looking like this," she said, standing up so he could see the full effect. She'd have to duck under doorways with this hair.

His myopic gaze flicked over her from head to toe. Then he shrugged. "The dress is a little dated, but I've seen worse."

"It's not my dress," she cried, feeling more self-conscious than ever as she smoothed down the skirt. "It's my hair. Look at it!"

He walked into the room, circling her as he stared at her hair. "Wow," he said with a grimace. "That's some head of hair. Justine must be on her mousse kick again. We had to take away her stash last year."

She breathed a sigh of relief that he finally understood her dilemma. "Well, I obviously can't go on looking like this. Can you reschedule me for tomorrow or sometime next week?"

Devon shook his head. "No way. You have to go on today, Dr. Grant. You're on the schedule and the schedule is sacred around here. This is television. We have to meticulously account for every second." He glanced at his watch again. "And you've only got two minutes and five seconds until showtime."

"You can give my time slot to the Jolly Greengrocer," she said a little desperately. "He can give an in-depth report on the fruit of the month. What is it this month?"

"The tomato," he said, as if reciting it by rote. "Sometimes called the love apple back in pioneer days. Once thought poisonous, today it is used in a variety of condiments around the world. The tomato is a versatile, meaty fruit that people often mistake for a vegetable."

"See," she said excitedly. "There's plenty to learn about the tomato. You could probably do an entire show on it."

"We did," he replied. "Two weeks ago. It was the Jolly Greengrocer's big finale. He's a goner. And so is the cooking lady. The show's got a whole new format since Midge took over—dealing with hot topics and issues that affect the good citizens of Pine City."

Stifling a groan, Rachel closed her eyes. After today's show, the hottest topic in town would be what she had hidden in her hair. "I can't believe this is happening to me."

"Wait," he said, moving in a step. "Let me see if I can fix it." He put the palm of his hand on top of her hair and pushed down. Hard. Then he lifted his hand and stepped back to look at the results.

"Is it better?" she asked hopefully.

"Well..." He cleared his throat. "You know, the audience really doesn't pay that much attention to hair once the show starts. Just smile a lot. You've got a very pretty smile. Then they'll focus on your face instead of"—he pointed to the top of her head —"that."

"Audience?" she echoed, looking frantically around the room for a mirror. "What

audience?

"That's new to the show, too. We've got a whole new look. Live audience. New set design. It's all very state-of-the art. Midge demands the best of everything."

Rachel steadied herself by taking deep, calming breaths. Maybe she did have a case of television jitters after all. This was just a local show. The audience probably consisted of a high school civics class on a field trip.

"You're on in forty-five seconds," Devon announced, propelling her toward the stage door. "Look on the bright side, Dr. Grant. Sometimes unusual hairstyles start a trend. You could be a real Pine City trendsetter."

Somehow Rachel doubted the women of Pine City would be running to the beauty shop to request Hurricane Hair. She followed Devon in the shadows until they reached the edge of the set.

It looked smaller than she'd imagined, with two overstuffed armchairs on a raised circular dais. The audience sat around the dais on wooden bleachers, five rows high, and buzzed with excitement.

Rachel stood motionless as Devon clipped a cordless microphone onto the collar of her dress. Music suddenly blared out of the big speaker next to her, making her jump.

The show had begun.

"Good afternoon, Pine City!" Midge shouted as took the stage. Sporting an aqua-blue pantsuit that matched her eyes, the sixty-one-year-old looked smart and stylish. "I'm Midge Berman and I want to welcome you to the best show in town!"

Neon applause signs flashed above the stage, and the audience responded enthusiastically. Midge smiled and clasped her hands together in appreciation.

Midge had every reason to smile, Rachel thought to herself as her palms began to sweat. Her silver-gray hair looked normal. Even attractive, arranged in a cute pixie cut. Justine and her magic mousse obviously hadn't been anywhere near her.

"With Valentine's Day coming up next week, we've decided to make the topic of this show, *Valentine's Day—Love it or Leave it*. And I'd like everyone to give a warm welcome to one of the best therapists in Pine City, Dr. Rachel Grant!"

"You're on!" Devon exclaimed amid the spattering of applause.

Surprised by Devon's gentle shove, Rachel stumbled onto the stage. Still, she forced herself to smile as she headed toward her chair, all too aware of the hot, bright lights and the camera lenses pointed in her direction. She silently reassured herself that this fiasco would soon be over.

And it might not be so bad. She could discuss some of the common myths about love and happiness. There were probably many people watching today's show who had mixed feelings about February the fourteeth. Maybe some members of the audience felt the same way as her group members.

Maybe they were already making snide comments about her hair.

"We're so happy to have you on the show today, Dr. Grant," Midge said, motioning her toward the guest chair.

"Thank you for the opportunity," Rachel replied as they both sat down. Her voice sounded tinny to her ears. Settling into her chair, she began to relax a little, until she caught a glimpse of herself in the monitor. To her horror, her hair looked even bigger on television.

Midge folded her hands in her lap, more serious now as she settled into the interview. "Tell us, Dr. Grant, do you hate men?"

Rachel blinked back her surprise. "No, not at all."

The audience applauded and Midge clapped along with them. "When I heard about your Lonely Hearts group boycotting Valentine's Day, I wasn't sure what to think. Can you explain it to us?"

"Of course," Rachel said, trying to mentally summon the information she'd memorized earlier. "Valentine's Day is a time for romance, and it's become very commercialized. They sell cards and heart-shaped candy boxes. And a florist told me once that it's her most profitable day of the year."

Midge looked confused. "And that's...bad?"

"Not at all. I'm very much in favor of romance. And of love. It's very important in our society. But when we blow that importance out of proportion, it can become difficult for people who are alone or depressed. They often feel like something's wrong with them." Rachel looked out at the audience. "What I try to impart to the members of the Lonely Hearts group is that if you love yourself first, happiness usually follows."

Midge nodded thoughtfully. "So this boycott of yours isn't personal? Or a result of a romance gone sour?"

Panic suddenly gripped her that Midge knew about Russell. *But knew what?* That he had abandoned her for an African dung beetle?

"No, of course it's not personal," Rachel replied.

"And it's not *my* boycott." Perspiration began to run down her brow. "It's simply about people having the choice to celebrate or *not* celebrate Valentine's Day. And to know that either decision is just fine."

"Thank you, Dr. Grant," Midge said, turning back to the camera. "Let's see what our audience members have to say about this very interesting issue."

Rachel breathed a silent sigh of relief that the interview part was over. Then she saw Devon holding a microphone up to a blond teenage girl.

"I think Valentine's Day is way cool," the girl said. "And maybe the doctor lady wouldn't have so much trouble finding a boyfriend if she did something different with her hair. No offense, you're probably very pretty but that hair has to go."

The audience applauded as Devon shoved the microphone in front of a middle-aged man wearing a Hooters T-shirt. "I like the hair. And she's got a great-looking body, too. I don't think she'd have any trouble finding a date for Valentine's Day."

Rachel's head began to throb. How soon until they went to commercial? Then maybe she could make a quick and dignified escape from this circus.

Midge winked at Rachel. "The folks in Pine City have strong opinions. And the voice in my earpiece is telling me we have a live caller with a question. Caller, go ahead."

"I've got a Valentine's message for Rachel," said a

weirdly distorted male voice. *"Roses are red, corpses are blue. Keep watch, my love, I'm coming for you."*

Rachel froze as stunned gasps sounded from the audience. She couldn't believe her stalker had just threatened to kill her on live television. "Who is this?" she asked, but her question was followed by a loud click.

"Oh, that's horrible," Midge murmured under her breath. Then she rallied and turned to Rachel. "I believe that caller may have been one of those people you were talking about. Someone who sounds disturbed...*highly disturbed* by Valentine's Day or some other serious issue. Do you have a response, Dr. Grant?"

Still shocked by what had just happened, Rachel automatically opened the file on her lap. "Midge, did you know statistics show that calls to mental health hotlines triple during the week before Valentine's Day? We need to remind people that they don't have to surrender to all the hype. That it's okay *not* to be in a relationship. And most important of all, that love is not a requirement for happiness."

"Well said," Marge exclaimed, leading the audience in applause. "It's clear now that this boycott isn't a personal vendetta of yours."

Rachel nodded, still functioning on auto-pilot after that call. "Of course not. I'm a romantic at heart. I love to read romance novels and watch a good love story on television."

"But what about romance in real life?"

"I'm all for it," she replied. "I enjoy dating." She knew Gina and Molly might disagree that assessment after the blind dates she'd bailed on. But she wasn't about to dissect her love life on live television. "And I certainly enjoy the company of men."

Midge smiled. "Actually, a little birdie told me you've just started dating a handsome veterinarian."

"Oh," Rachel said, aware of whispers in the studio audience. "Yes, I am. His name is Dr. Hank Holden."

"Then we have a surprise for you," Midge announced, beaming into the camera. "Come on out, Dr. Holden!"

Rachel's mouth dropped open as Hank walked out of the wings carrying a bouquet of purple calla lilies.

He walked right up to her, looking impeccably handsome in a western style gray suit and matching cowboy hat.

"Surprise," he said with a wry smile. Then his gaze flicked up somewhere above her eyebrows. "What happened to your hair?"

❀ 9 ❀

Hank held the calla lilies out to Rachel, wanting to kick himself.

What happened to your hair? Smooth, Holden. Very smooth.

And on live television, too. Besides, her hair didn't look that bad. It was a little poofy. And kind of flat on top. But he liked the way it made her appear taller and statuesque.

Even with that hair, Dr. Rachel Grant was a knockout.

But the way she was staring daggers at him now made him regret arranging to surprise her on the show. At the time, he'd thought it would be a good way to attract the attention of her stalker.

But after receiving an emergency call from Charlie, who needed help with a difficult birth of twin foals, he'd just made it to the studio in time to hear Midge call him onto the stage.

"These are for you," he said, hoping she'd just play along for the camera.

Midge squealed. *"Ooob,* just look at those beautiful flowers!" She turned to the camera. "Courtesy of Fiorelli's Florist at Ninth and Baltic. Fiorelli's can make your Valentine's Day a rosy one. Stop in and take advantage of their Sweetheart Specials."

Hank inched the bouquet closer to Rachel, feeling even more foolish when she folded her arms across her chest and glared at him. How long did she expect him to stand there looking like an idiot?

"Don't they make a cute couple?" Midge gushed, while the audience hooted and clapped. "For those of us who speak the language of flowers, purple calla lilies represent passionate love."

At last, Rachel took the bouquet from him, but she didn't seem happy about it.

"The sparks are flying, folks," Midge said, looking between the two of them. Then she held a microphone out to Hank. "I believe you had something you wanted to ask Dr. Grant."

He cleared his throat. "Rachel, will you be my Valentine?"

Midge turned her megawatt smile on Rachel. "How about it, Dr. Grant? Do you accept Dr. Holden's offer?"

He didn't understand why Rachel looked so upset. They'd agreed to a fake romance and been out in public as a couple several times. Maybe she just had stage fright, but he sensed there was something more behind her tense expression.

The audience grew fidgety as the silence stretched between them. Hank held his breath as he awaited her answer.

"It sounds like an offer I can't refuse," Rachel said at last, leading the audience to burst into applause.

"Wonderful!" Midge boomed into the microphone. "And Rawlings Steakhouse is happy to sponsor a lovely Valentine's Day dinner for these two fledgling lovebirds. Congratulations!"

The audience rose to their feet, still applauding, as Midge ended the show.

Hank hugged her and whispered, "This should get your stalker's attention."

Her lips brushed against his ear. "I think he just threatened to kill me."

"What do you mean he called the show?" Hank asked.

Rachel sat in the passenger seat of his pickup truck, watching the scenery roll by as he drove to her house. She'd walked out of the television studio only to find both rear tires of her car had been slashed. Hank had handled calling a tire repair service, but it would be at least a two-hour wait and neither one of them wanted to hang around that long for her stalker's amusement.

"Midge let the audience comment during my segment, including a live caller," she explained. "That's when he recited his verse." She shook her head, still chilled by the memory. *"Roses are red, corpses are blue. Keep watch, my love, I'm coming for you."*

She watched Hank's large hands tighten on the steering wheel, then he made a hard left, causing her to lean into the door. "What are you doing?"

"Taking you to Elk Creek Ranch," he said as they headed north out of Pine City. "Grandma Hattie has her book club meeting tonight, but I know she'll agree to have you stay there for as long as we need. I want you out of sight until we catch this maniac."

She watched as they passed the last of the streetlights and the paved street turned into a country road. The rumble of the tires on gravel made her realize how far away she was from home. "Maybe I should go back to Philly instead."

"You mean to visit?"

"No, I mean permanently." She shifted in the passenger seat so she was half facing Hank. "I know we've talked about it before, but what if he doesn't stop? You have to go back to your life. And I have to live mine without looking over my shoulder all the time."

"Do you want to move back to Pennsylvania?"

"No, I don't. I love it here. I've got a great practice at the Craig Clinic and I'd have to start all over in Philly. And as much as I miss my family, I feel like this is where I belong."

She took a deep breath, realizing the shock of the stalker's threat was evolving into a determination not to let him win. "Turn around, Hank, and take me home. I refuse to run away."

"It's not running, it's keeping you safe."

"I can take care of myself. Please, just turn around."

Hank's mouth tightened, but he did as she asked. Soon, they were on the way back into Pine City.

For the next several miles, they sat in silence. Rachel sensed he was trying to formulate a persuasive argument to change her mind. But she'd already allowed the stalker too much influence over her life—including her fake romance with Hank.

She watched him now as he traversed the road, his cowboy hat shading his eyes from the late afternoon sun. "Why didn't you tell me you were coming to the studio? Did Midge blackmail you too?"

"No," he said, glancing over at her. "I called her, thinking if I showed up with flowers and asked you to be my Valentine, it might trigger the stalker into acting out. Of course, I had no idea he'd act out all on his own."

Rachel suddenly sat up in the seat. "But that's what we want, right? For him to keep acting out." She looked at Hank. "I need to be bait."

He scowled. "I don't like the sound of that."

"No, listen! I can take care of myself. We need to give him a chance to approach me when no one else is around. Or when he *thinks* no one else is around."

Hank pulled into her driveway and cut the engine, then opened his door.

"I think that's the worst idea I've ever heard."

She followed him up the sidewalk. The more she thought about it, the more Rachel was willing to risk it. "I think we've been going about this the wrong way," she told him, unlocking the front door and walking inside.

Georgie ran up to greet them, wriggling with excitement.

"Most stalkers are very insecure," she continued. "Stalking someone makes them feel powerful. But you exude power and confidence, Hank. I think he'd find that very intimidating and take pains to avoid you."

Hank knelt down to pet the dog. "So then what's the answer?"

She met his gaze. "We break up in a public place. And go our separate ways."

"Wow, you're full of terrible ideas today." He walked to the kitchen and filled the dog's water bowl. "I'm not going anywhere when that creep is still out there. He just slashed your tires!"

"I know." Rachel followed him into the kitchen, realizing the most difficult part of this new plan might be convincing Hank to go along with it. "So let me rephrase the plan. We'll *pretend* to go our separate ways. I want him to think I'm alone and vulnerable. That's when he'll approach me."

Hank shook his head. "I don't get your logic. He didn't approach you before we started our fake romance."

Another possibility dawned on her. "Yes, he did. He got close to me when he left that note in my coat pocket. He just didn't approach me directly. But that same night is when we kissed in the lobby and we've been together ever since."

Hank looked thoughtful. "You may be right. If he was the one driving that red Buick, he could have been trying to determine if you were alone that night I saw him." He took off his cowboy hat and raked a hand through his hair. "I don't know—we're really just guessing."

"Let's just give it a try. With any luck, he'll approach me as soon as he sees us break up and he thinks I'm on my own. We just need to figure out where to do it."

"I think I know the perfect place." He smiled. "I'll pick you up tomorrow night at eight."

"Okay," she said, determined to make it work.

The chime of the doorbell brought Georgie running to the front door, barking all the way.

"Hold on, girl, let me answer." Rachel walked toward the door as the doorbell rang three more times in quick succession.

"All right, already," she muttered, pulling the door open. Then her knees almost buckled, because standing in front of her was a tall bearded man with shaggy blond hair that hung almost to his shoulders and a worn khaki knapsack slung over one shoulder. A man she barely recognized.

"Russell?" she gasped.

The man in the doorway grinned at her. "Hi, honey, I'm home."

Hank didn't know which bothered him more: the way this character sashayed into the house as if he lived here, or the way Rachel let him. She was still holding the front door open, as if she'd just seen someone return from the dead.

Unfortunately, Russell Baker was very much alive. Scruffy, but alive. And he had that rugged mountain man look that some women fell for.

But judging by Georgie's deep, suspicious growl and the way her ears were drawn all the way back, she wasn't impressed with him either. In Hank's experience, dogs were some of the best judges of character.

Hank knew he should call off his dog, but this was the man who had abandoned Rachel and broken her heart, so he deserved to be growled at.

Russell hesitated, looking between Rachel and the dog. "Does she bite?"

"It depends," Rachel told him as she gently led the dog away from Russell and into the living room. Then she leaned down to pet her. "It's okay, girl. Russell's a friend."

"More than a friend, actually," Russell said, following them. Then he dropped his knapsack on the sofa and swept Rachel up in his arms, whirling her around in a big bear hug. "You look wonderful, Lovebug."

Lovebug?

A swift and totally unexpected jab of jealousy sucker-punched Hank in the gut. He barely resisted the overwhelming urge to grab this guy by the scruff of his neck and toss him out into the street.

Probably not the most diplomatic way for him to handle the situation, but he wasn't feeling particularly diplomatic at the moment. Especially since the guy looked as if he'd just come in on the last train.

His thick blond hair, though neatly combed now,

hung almost to his shoulders. A heavy growth of golden whiskers covered his square jaw. He wore faded blue jeans and a wrinkled button-up shirt under a weathered pea jacket. Only his shoes looked as if they hadn't come from a thrift shop: a brand-new pair of hiking boots.

But Rachel didn't seem to care about his rumpled appearance. She just kept staring at him. At last, she said, "Russell, what on earth are you doing here?"

Hank folded his arms across his chest, patiently awaiting the answer to that excellent question.

"I couldn't wait to see you," Russell explained. "So I just came here straight from the airport. It was a long, exhausting trip, but those international flights always are." He looked around the house, nodding his approval. "The place still looks great. And so do you."

That seemed to shake her out of her daze. "Oh... thank you. Would you like something to drink? Some coffee or tea?"

"No, I don't want you go to any trouble," Russell said, his eyes lingering on her. "I just want to drink you in, Rachel. It's been so long."

Despite the fact that they both seemed to have forgotten his existence, Hank had no intention of making a discreet exit. He moved to the sofa, deftly throwing the guy's knapsack onto the floor, and then settled in for a long stay. "Don't mind me, you two go ahead and catch up."

She tore her gaze from Russell and blinked at Hank. He had the distinct feeling she'd forgotten he was there. The sudden reappearance of her ex had truly rattled her.

"Oh, I'm sorry," she said at last. "Russell, this is Hank Holden. He's my..."

"Boyfriend." Hank finished the introduction for her, wanting Russell to know exactly where he stood in the pecking order.

Russell cocked an eyebrow. "Really? That surprises me. You don't strike me as Rachel's type."

"And who exactly are you?" Hank asked, playing along. Because Rachel had never said one word to him about Russell. He only knew about him because he'd eavesdropped on the Lonely Hearts group before joining them and heard about the way Russell had abandoned her on the most romantic day of the year.

Rachel cleared her throat. "This is Russell Baker. He's my..."

"Fiancé," Russell concluded with a cocky grin.

Hank turned to Rachel. "You're engaged?"

"Yes. No. Well...I suppose, technically, we're sort of engaged."

Hank's jaw clenched, his voice sounding harsher than he intended. "Rachel, there's no such thing as *sort of* engaged. Either you're engaged or you're not."

Rachel tipped up her chin. "You're right. We're

not engaged," she said in a firmer voice. "Not anymore."

"But, Lovebug..." Russell began.

"Please don't call me that." She turned to him. "I've never liked that nickname. And how dare you waltz into my house one year after you waltzed out, without a word or a letter or even a telephone call."

"I can explain."

Hank sat back, ready to enjoy the show. He knew from personal experience that nobody could do battle like Rachel Grant.

"Explain?" she repeated, her green eyes snapping. "How do you explain practically abandoning me at the altar? We were supposed to get married last spring. Until you pulled your disappearing act."

Married? Last spring? The words hit Hank like a shotgun blast to the heart.

A gentleman would leave these two alone to work out their problems. Then again, a gentleman wouldn't have kissed Rachel to the point of passing out. So maybe he should stay. It was his job to protect her, after all. And as far as he was concerned, that job description wasn't limited to stalkers.

"Just hear me out, Lovebug," Russell said.

Hank's hand curled into a fist. If he called her that stupid pet name one more time...

"I mean Rachel," Russell amended, quickly correcting himself.

"All right," she said, settling into the chair, a ruddy flush on her cheeks. "Let's hear it."

Russell began to pace back and forth in front of her. "Let me take you back to last February," he began, "so you can be inside my head."

That was the last place Hank wanted to be, but Rachel actually looked intrigued. He supposed that was the therapist in her. Which made him wonder if Russell knew just what buttons to push.

"I didn't have any doubts about our marrying until I was awarded that grant from the entomology department. You remember that day?"

She nodded. "We celebrated with champagne."

"And suddenly I had enough money for my dream trip to Africa to study the dung beetle." Russell took a deep sip of wine. "Only, how could I ask you to give up your career and come with me? You were a rising star in your field—everybody said so. And I couldn't imagine getting married and then spending our honeymoon apart. Especially since I'd be gone for months."

"So you chose the dung beetle over me," Rachel said softly.

"I needed to find myself," Russell explained. "I didn't know what I wanted anymore. I wasn't sure I was ready for marriage. And I loved you too much to pretend."

Hank rolled his eyes, but Rachel seemed spellbound. She pulled her long legs up against her chest, wrapping her arms around them and resting her chin on her knees.

Russell sighed. "But instead of finding myself, I got lost."

"You mean emotionally lost?" Rachel asked.

Russell shook his head. "No, I mean actually lost. One of the guides took me into the bush on a beetle safari. But it started to rain, a downpour actually, and the Jeep got stuck in the mud. While the guide went to get help, I went in search of shelter. My colleagues finally found me six months later, living in a remote village."

"That's...incredible," Rachel said.

Hank found it preposterous. This so-called story sounded more like a pile of...dung. But Rachel actually looked as if she believed him. Or wanted to believe him.

"It was crazy," Russell acknowledged. "But you can check it out with Professor Simmons from the university. They were all ready to give me up for dead when they came upon me in that village three weeks ago."

"Lucky for us," Hank said dryly.

"Getting lost in the bush was the best thing that ever happened to me." Russell gazed into Rachel's eyes. "Not only did I discover a rare new species of African dung beetle, but I discovered I loved you,

Rachel. Truly and deeply. And now the most important thing to me is spending the rest of my life making you happy."

She twisted her hands in her lap. "This is all so... unexpected. I don't know what to say." "You don't have to say anything," Russell assured her. Then he looked at

Hank, hitching his eyebrows toward the door. Sending him a silent message to get lost himself.

Hank just smiled as he settled deeper into the sofa. He wasn't planning on going anywhere.

Russell gave up and turned back to Rachel. He pulled a small velvet box out of his knapsack. "This is for you," he said, handing it to her.

She held it in her hands, looking uncertain. "Gee, Russell, you shouldn't have."

"Open it," he prodded.

Hank set his jaw, wondering if Russell dressed like a drifter because he'd spent all his cash on a three-carat diamond ring. Or some exquisite emerald from an African mine.

He carefully watched Rachel's expression as she opened the lid. If she smiled and squealed at the sight of some gaudy ring, then Hank was out the door.

But instead of joy, her face reflected puzzlement. Rachel looked up at Russell. "It's a bug."

He bent down in front of her. "I know. The rare dung beetle I discovered near that village. Unknown until now, it's destined to make me famous among entomologists all over the world."

She stared down at the dead black bug in the red velvet box. "That's...wonderful, Russell."

"But you haven't even heard the best part," he exclaimed.

"You're going back to Africa?" Hank ventured.

Russell scowled at him, then turned back to Rachel. "No. The best part is that I named it for you. You're looking at the *Rachelona cyanella*."

Her eyes widened as she stared at the beetle. "I don't know what to say."

Russell moved closer to her, grasping her free hand in both of his. "Say you'll take me back, Rachel. Please let me prove to you how much I really love you."

When his chest began aching, Hank realized he was holding his breath waiting for her answer. On the one hand, he thought Rachel was much too sensible to fall for this guy's lame stories. On the other hand, she'd loved him once. Maybe she still did.

Russell took the velvet box from her, carefully closing it, then setting it on an end table. "You don't have to answer right now. I know this is all a shock to you. I probably should have called you as soon as I got back to the States. But I wrote you a letter every day I spent in that village." He pulled out a stack of ivory envelopes tied with a pink silk ribbon from his knapsack.

"They have hotel stationery in the bush?" Hank asked, not bothering to hide his skepticism.

"I wrote it on tree bark, then transcribed it onto paper later." He pushed the envelopes into her lap. "You can read these, then give me your answer. We'll have plenty of time to get reacquainted now that I'm back."

"Where are you staying?" Rachel asked.

Russell put on a little-boy-lost expression that he'd obviously perfected wandering around in Africa. "I spent my last dime on the airline ticket. I couldn't wait to be with you again. But since I won't start teaching back at the university until the summer session, I was hoping you'd let me camp out here."

"Here?" Rachel and Hank said at the same time.

"I travel light," he said, motioning to his knapsack. "I've learned to relinquish material things for what's really important, like love and friendship. I just want to fill my life and my heart with you."

Hank thought he might be sick. What did this guy do, memorize greeting cards in his spare time?

Rachel nibbled her lower lip. "I have a lot going on in my life right now..."

"I know," Russell said. "But I don't have anywhere else to go."

For the first time, it occurred to Hank that

Russell might be her stalker. Maybe he'd planned to scare her into wanting him back. The guy seemed just cocky enough to come up with a plan that would make him a hero.

Just that long-shot possibility made him want to wipe that smile off Russell's face. Preferably with his fist. But what right did he have to interfere with their relationship? Despite the time Hank had spent with her—and the kisses they'd shared—he didn't have any claim on Rachel. He'd never wanted a relationship with any woman.

But that didn't mean he'd throw her to a wolf like Russell.

He looked from Rachel to her fast-talking ex-fiancé as a new strategy formed in his mind. He didn't like it. Hell, he hadn't even thought it all the way through yet. But he could see Rachel wavering. He needed to act fast. He needed to keep Russell away from her.

He needed...a roommate.

❧ 10 ❦

"Wait, what? You want me to babysit an entomologist?" Katie sat at the computer in Hank's home office, her fingers flying over the keyboard.

She'd been a tomboy growing up, but she'd grown out her thick blond hair and traded her softball cleats for fashionable heels. "I thought you called me over here to analyze a phone call."

"It would be great if you could do both," he told his cousin. "I also told Russell you'd help him download some of his bug pictures on my computer so he can enlarge them." Hank buttoned the cuff of his shirt, a sinking feeling in the pit of his stomach about the evening ahead.

Rachel was bound and determined to go through

with a fake breakup so she could be bait for the stalker. It had trouble written all over it.

To make matters worse, Russell had established some kind of bug colony in Hank's spare bedroom. There was no doubt he really loved bugs of all shapes and sizes. The question in Hank's mind was if Russell really loved Rachel. Because there was just something about the guy he didn't trust.

"It sounds like I have a fun evening ahead," Katie told him. "You're going to owe me, Hank."

"I know," he said with a sigh.

She smiled up at him. "I do have the recording ready to go if you want to listen to it."

"I do," he said, impressed with her skills.

A cowgirl with an affinity for computers was a rare commodity in this part of Texas, but at twenty-six, Katie managed to excel at both. Like most Holden kin, she had a love of horses, an independent spirit, and a stubborn streak the length of a country mile.

Since she'd already taken a job for Cowboy Confidential, he felt comfortable confiding in her about his duty to protect Rachel from a stalker—and from her ex-fiancé.

He also wanted to see if they might be the same person. It just seemed too coincidental that Russell would appear right when her stalker was starting to escalate. Rachel had dismissed the idea, but Hank wasn't so sure.

"Okay," Katie said, pressing a button. "Here you go."

A moment later, Hank heard a distorted male voice say, "*Roses are red, corpses are blue. Keep watch, my love. I'm coming for you.*"

Katie's eyes widened as she looked up at him. "Well, that's one of the creepiest things I've ever heard."

"And a clear danger to her," Hank said. The threat in the man's tone was unmistakable and even more chilling than he'd imagined.

"This guy's after your Dr. Grant?" Katie began typing rapidly on the keyboard. "Do you have any clue who it is?"

"None so far. That's what makes this all so frustrating. The cops are looking into it, but there's got to be something I can do."

Katie turned and craned her neck to look at him. "Wow, you're really taking this job seriously. I've never seen you so dedicated to a woman before."

"To a client," he corrected her. "I'm just trying to keep her safe."

"Right." Katie looked back at the computer screen and shook her head. "So, who's protecting Dr. Grant right now?"

He rubbed his forehead, feeling another headache

coming on. "No one, that's the problem. She wants the stalker to approach her and believes he won't do that if I'm around. We're about to have a very public breakup at the Wildcat Tavern in about an hour."

"That doesn't like a great idea to me."

"Tell me about it." The problem for Hank was that Rachel didn't agree. But he couldn't do anything about it. And he knew they had to do something. Because he'd go back to work at the vet clinic in two weeks, and then Rachel would be completely on her own.

A shout suddenly erupted from the second floor.

"Speaking of weird," Hank said, looking over at the staircase. "You're about to meet my number one suspect in this stalker case."

Before he could explain, Russell bounded down the stairs two steps at a time. He looked bedraggled and wild-eyed, his flannel shirt hanging out of his jeans. He skidded to a stop at the bottom of the stairs, hanging on to the banister for support.

"What's the problem now?" Hank asked him.

"My *Megaloblatta longipennis,*" he said. "It's gone."

"And what is that?"

"It's the largest cockroach in the world," Russell explained, pacing back and forth. "It's from Japan and very rare. We have to call the police."

Katie shot up from her chair. "A giant cockroach? Forget the police, I'm calling an exterminator. If a large insect gets inside a computer, it can cause a short circuit and all kinds of damage."

"Don't worry, Katie, all of Russell's bugs are dead."

"Most of them," Russell amended. "Not all."

Katie rolled her eyes as she sat back down in the chair. "I don't get what all the fuss is about."

Russell walked over to her. "I have the most extensive cockroach collection in the country. The *Megaloblatta longipennis* is the crowning jewel, coveted by all my colleagues." He pulled a cell phone out of his pocket. "One of them probably stole it. Just another case of entomologist envy. I'm calling the cops."

"Wait a minute, Russ," Hank said, looking around the room. "Are you sure you didn't lose it somewhere?"

Russell raked his hand through his blond hair. "Of course not. I always keep it in the special locked case with the rest of the collection. I left it open last night and now the Megaloblatta is gone." Nacho the cat suddenly scampered around the corner, tossing a suspicious brown object in the air with her paw.

Russell looked on in horror. "My Megaloblatta!" He caught it in midair, then checked it for damage. Finally, he breathed a long sigh of relief. "Miraculously it seems to be in good condition."

Hank wished he could say the same about Katie, who looked more than a little green around the gills.

He turned to Russell. "Maybe you'd better take it back upstairs and put it away. You can lock the case in your bedroom closet for safekeeping. Just don't lose the key."

"I'll guard it with my life," Russell said, cradling the dead bug in his hands as he ascended the staircase.

Katie sank down onto the sofa. "Who is that guy? Don't tell me he's a friend of yours."

"Not exactly. He's Russell Baker, a soon-to-be famous entomologist, according to him.

Also known as Rachel's ex-fiancé."

Katie held up one hand. "Your Rachel?"

"She's not *my* Rachel," Hank said, even though that's exactly how he'd been thinking of her. Especially after Russell had arrived and tried to stake his claim. He'd spent enough time with the bug man to know he was definitely the wrong man for Rachel. "Russell took off a year ago, on Valentine's Day, and then he just showed up on her doorstep last night."

"Wow, that takes some nerve."

"No kidding," Hank agreed. "Now he's back with some cockamamie story, claiming he's madly in love with her. He even planned on moving in with her."

Katie tipped her head to one side. "But you invited him to stay at your place instead?"

"I thought it was safer," he explained.

She arched a brow. "And a good way to keep tabs on your competition?"

Hank ignored the question. "I still can't believe Russell thought he could show up on Rachel's doorstep and she'd welcome him with open arms."

Katie leaned forward in her chair. "So how did she react?"

"I think she was shocked." He tugged at the collar of his shirt. "And more understanding than I would be in that situation. But here's my question: what does she see in the guy? Because he's a mess."

"A hot mess," she said, watching Russell walk up the stairs. "Hot being the operative word. He's got that sexy professor vibe going for him. And even if he's a little eccentric, he's clearly a very handsome man."

Hank frowned. "That's your answer?"

She gave him a sympathetic smile. "If he was her first love, then it's hard to let go of that ideal. It's possible she doesn't see the same Russell that you and I see."

That's not what he wanted to hear, but he knew Katie spoke from experience. She'd been engaged right after high school, but eventually broke it off. As far as he knew, she hadn't been serious about any man since.

He pointed to her computer. "Any luck analyzing that call from the stalker?"

"All I can tell you is that it came from a local number and it's a landline phone, not a cell."

"How did you find that information?"

She met his gaze. "It's better if you don't know my methods. Then you have plausible deniability."

"Okay, but just make sure you stay out of trouble or Grandma Hattie will have my head."

She laughed. "Don't worry, I never get caught." Then she grew more serious. "Do you have any leads at all about Rachel's stalker? It has to be someone she knows, doesn't it?"

"That's the most likely scenario. And Rachel follows a pretty regular daily routine. She's either at her home, her office building, or a place called Bonnie's Diner that's located close to her office building. But she's also got a long list of blind dates from the past few months, so it's taking a while to check them all out. But so far there are no likely candidates."

"Well, I'll keep looking for clues online. Maybe I'll come across something in a local chatroom."

"Thanks, I appreciate it. And can you keep an eye on Russell until I get back?" He walked over to the hall tree and grabbed his black cowboy hat. "You don't have to interact with him; I just want to know if he leaves and at what time."

"Got it," she said, following him to the door. "And good luck with your breakup!"

"What's wrong with my dress?" Rachel asked as they walked into the Wildcat Tavern.

He gently clasped her bare arm as they made their way through the crowd. "Nothing's wrong it."

"Then why do you keep glaring at it?" She smoothed one hand over the short, flirty skirt. "I've received a lot of criticism lately that my fashion choices are too dated. So I'm trying to go in the other direction."

"You look great," he bit out, already aware of the stares she was getting as he searched the room for an empty table. One thing was certain—she'd definitely grab the attention of her stalker if he was here tonight. She had the attention of every man in the joint.

They'd met in the parking lot, after driving here separately, and gone over their plan once more. At some point in the evening, they'd have a spat, then Rachel would drive off alone. Hank would soon follow her in the SUV he'd borrowed from Charlie earlier today. His job was to be on the lookout for anything suspicious without calling attention to himself.

"Where did you get that dress?" he asked. "It's not your usual style."

"I searched online for a dress that looks good

with cowboy boots. I wanted make sure I fit in tonight."

"You fit in," he assured her, grasping her arm just a little tighter. He was having serious second thoughts about using her as bait to entice her stalker.

Several of the patrons hailed him, and a few gave him a thumbs-up when they saw him with Rachel. Then he caught sight of an empty table and headed in that direction. A live band played country music and several couples filled the dance floor.

"Hey there!" Lacie said, walking up to them with a notepad in her hand. She wore the unofficial Wildcat uniform of a tiger-striped peasant blouse and blue jeans, complete with a cowboy hat and boots. "It's nice to see you two." She gave them a coy smile. "Are you on a date?"

"Um...maybe," Rachel said, suddenly looking uncomfortable. "I mean, we're together but..."

"Yes, we've started dating," Hank interjected. "I'm not her patient, so it's all good."

Lacie's face fell as she looked at Hank. "Does this mean you won't be coming to any more Lonely Hearts group meetings?"

He shook his head. "I feel like that first meeting cleared everything up for me." He glanced at Rachel. "It's like I'm a new man."

"Well, that's no surprise," Lacie said. "Steven told me she's the best therapist in town." Then she blushed. "We've gone out to lunch a couple times," she said, referring to the clinic's receptionist. "He's so smart and funny."

Rachel nodded her approval. "I think he's a good one."

Relief shone in Lacie's brown eyes. "Me too." Then she pulled a pen out of her pocket. "What can I get you to start?"

Rachel looked around the table. "Are there menus?"

Hank pointed to the chalkboard above the long, polished oak bar. "You'll find everything they serve on that board. It changes week to week."

"Oh, fun," she said, smiling as she scanned the chalkboard. "I'll just have a glass of Merlot."

"And I'll take a coffee," Hank said.

Lacie stared at him. "That's it? Just a coffee?"

"That's it." While he'd normally order a beer to celebrate the weekend, he was still under orders not to drink alcohol. But even if he wasn't, Hank wanted to be fully alert for what might lie ahead.

After Lacie left, Hank scooted his chair closer to Rachel and draped one arm around her back. "We need to put on a good show," he said, slowly scanning the room. "Do you see anyone you recognize?"

"No, I don't think so. I hope this isn't a big waste of time."

He cupped her bare shoulder with his right hand. "Hey, even if your stalker's not here yet, he might be on his way. Or outside, waiting for you."

She laughed. "I can't believe we're hoping my stalker is here. That sounds nuts."

"Not when we're planning to catch him. Then this can all be over."

Rachel leaned into him, resting her head on his shoulder. "That would be nice. You probably had no idea what you signed up for when you agreed to help me flush out the man stalking me."

He rested his cheek on the top of her head, finding it much too alluring to resist. Her silky hair smelled like apples and vanilla, and his fingers traced small circles on her bare shoulder.

"This is a busy place," Rachel mused.

"It can get pretty rowdy." He reached into his pocket as Lacie arrived with their beverages and set them on the table. Then he handed her a twenty-dollar bill. "Keep the change."

Lacie's eyes widened in appreciation. "Thank you! You two let me know if you need anything else."

After she left, Rachel looked up at Hank. "Do you think he's here?"

"Maybe," he said, assessing the crowd. It was filling up fast. "Let's go to the dance floor. It's elevated, so we can get a better view. You might recognize someone or see them watching you."

They made their way to the dance floor, Hank leading the way and holding Rachel's hand as they wove their way in and out of the growing crowd. Suddenly, her hand was yanked out of his. He quickly turned, but he couldn't see her in the crowd of bodies.

"Rachel!" he shouted.

But she was gone.

Rachel hit the floor hard, dazing her for a moment. A forest of legs surrounded her as the crowd milled around her. Then she looked up to see a familiar face staring down at her, his features contorted in anger.

"What makes you...think," Tad Grothen asked, slurring his words, "that you can just walk out on me?"

As she lay on the floor, she saw he wasn't wearing his toupee and his bared teeth revealed that he hadn't flossed recently. "You're drunk."

Tad stood over her, his feet on either side of her hips as he bent low to hurl invectives. "And then...you show up with some other guy a week later!"

"Get away from me." She tried to scoot away from him on the sticky floor. At last, she made it to her feet, but he grabbed her by one arm.

"You're just...a tease...aren't you," he stammered,

his dark eyes glazed as he looked her up and down. "Coming here in that dress." Then he reached out and grabbed her other arm, his fingers curling around it. "We're going to finish our date...right now...and you're going to...dance with me."

Rachel tried to pull away, but his fingers dug into her flesh as they stood face-to-face. "You should let go of me now," she warned him. "For your own good."

"For my own good?" He laughed. "There's not one cowpoke in here who can take me."

That's when she saw Hank hurtling toward them with an expression on his face that told her Tad was about to be pulverized. But she worried Tad might make it difficult for him and land a punch on Hank. She couldn't let him take that risk—not with his concussion.

"Sorry," she told Tad, who still had her in his grip. Then she quickly headbutted him, her forehead hitting him hard, right on the bridge of his nose.

He yelped in pain, releasing her as he stumbled backwards, blood dripping from his nose. "You broke my nose, you dumb..." The last word was silenced when he backed right into Hank.

"Going somewhere?" Hank picked him up like a sack of feed and pushed him hard against the wall. "If you ever put your hands on her again," he snarled, "you'll live to regret it. Because I can castrate you with my eyes closed." Then he looked over at Rachel. "Are you all right?"

The raw anger and passion she saw on his face sent a quiver through her. "Yes, I'm fine. Really. You should let him go."

"I'll think about it." He glowered at Tad, who held both hands to his bleeding nose as he dangled helplessly from Hank's grasp. Then he dropped him to the floor.

"You'll be sorry," Tad retorted, stumbling to maintain his balance before running for the door.

Everyone around them stood staring at the spectacle. Some of the crowd shouted angrily at Tad as he fled, then cheered when the bouncer caught him and prevented him from leaving.

A tap on her shoulder made Rachel turn around. She saw Lacie staring at her with both awe and regret.

"I'm sorry, Dr. Grant," Lacie said. "But my manager just called the cops about the fighting. Now all three of you are supposed to wait outside for them to arrive."

❧ 11 ❧

"These are nice benches," Rachel said, running her hand over the smooth wooden armrest fashioned out of a wagon wheel. Then she looked up into the night sky and the glittering canopy of stars above them. If she wasn't facing possible assault charges, it would be a perfect moment.

Hank sat next to her, staring daggers at Tad, who had been deposited on the other bench by the bouncer and ordered not to bleed on it.

Tad muttered to himself as he sat with his head tipped back and a handkerchief held to his bloody nose.

"You got what you deserved," Hank told him. "You should never put your hands on any woman like that—doesn't matter how much you've had to drink. I just wish I'd gotten to you first."

"Leave me alone," Tad grumbled, turning his back to them.

Rachel stared up at the sky, enjoying the peace and quiet out here compared to the raucous crowd inside. "I guess our plan didn't work out too well."

Hank chuckled. "I guess not. So tell me, where did you learn to headbutt like that?"

"My dad taught me." She smiled, remembering all the defensive lessons he'd given her. "He used to be a bouncer at a dance club when he was young, so he knew a lot of moves. He always told me the key to a good headbutt was to aim for the bridge of the nose with your forehead, because it's a soft target. Hitting forehead to forehead just risks knocking both people out."

"I'll try to remember that." He placed his arm loosely around her. "I'm just glad you're all right. When you disappeared..."

She leaned into him. "You thought my stalker had gotten to me?"

"Yeah," he said, his voice rough. "And I didn't like that feeling one bit."

Rachel looked into his blue eyes. "I've been telling you that I can take care of myself. Now do you believe me?" She smiled at him. "Like they say, you can take the girl out of Philly, but you can't take Philly out of the girl."

His mouth curved up in a half smile. "I guess I

should have listened to you. I just wished you'd have let me handle it."

"And risk you're getting another head injury?" she said in disbelief. "No way. I was trying to protect you."

"But that's my job."

She stared at him for a long moment. "You keep saying that, but it's not part of our agreement."

He started to speak, but an older woman with silver hair and bifocals bustled up to them. She looked about seventy and carried a large tote bag with the words *Bluebonnet Book Club* printed on it. "There you are."

"Grandma Hattie, what are you doing here?" he asked.

"Well, I heard you were at it again, Hank. So, what happened this time?"

Hank hitched his thumb in Tad's direction. "That guy started it." Then he motioned toward Rachel. "And she finished it, so I'm completely innocent."

"Well, that's a first," Hattie said, then smiled at Rachel. "Hello, I'm Hattie Holden, Hank's grandmother. I'm always happy to meet the young ladies in my grandsons' lives."

"Hello," Rachel said, standing up to introduce herself. "I'm Rachel Grant."

Hattie beamed at her. "Dr. Rachel Grant. I've

heard so much about you from my dear friends, Edith Cummings and Midge Berman. In fact, folks say you're the best therapist in the county."

"Oh, I don't know about that."

Hattie clucked her tongue. "Oh, honey, now don't be modest. You should always let your light shine bright."

Rachel laughed. "Okay, I'll try to remember that."

Then Hattie reached into her tote and pulled out a decorative glass bottle filled with a dark liquid. "Now if you two will excuse me, I need to deliver this to the bartender. He's always gets a bottle of my homemade blackberry cordial if he calls me when one of boys is in trouble."

"You're still bribing people around town with your cordial?" Hank asked in disbelief.

"I sure am," Hattie told him. "It started when you turned twenty-one, and here I am fourteen years later, still sticking to my end of the bargain." Her blue eyes twinkled as she looked at Rachel. "My boys might all be grown now, but they still keep me own my toes."

The flashing red light of a police car appeared in the distance and Rachel watched it pull into the long driveway leading up to the tavern.

"You two take care now," Hattie said as she made her way inside the building.

Rachel turned to Hank. "I like your grandmother. Let's just hope we don't go to jail tonight."

They watched as two young female officers emerged from the police car and started walking toward them.

"We're not going to jail," Hank assured her. "Tad put his hands on you first, so it was self-defense. And I," he continued woefully, "didn't even land one punch."

By the time the police finished taking all their stories, Rachel was relieved to discover that Hank was right. Rachel declined to press charges against Tad, figuring he was suffering enough from a cracked nose and bruised ego. So the cops let them all go.

While she was waiting for Hank to let his grandmother know what happened, Tad walked over to her and held out his hand.

"I just want to apologize," he said meekly. "I had too much to drink and lost control. It won't happen again."

Even though he'd been a jerk, she gave him a little credit for owning up to his bad behavior. Reaching out to shake his hand, she said, "I'm sorry, too. I hope you heal quickly."

"Thank you." Then still clasping her hand, he leaned in close enough to whisper in her ear. "You're a fool if you think Hank Holden is into you. Parker

Loomis told me his wife and another friend of yours secretly hired this guy to protect you from some stalker. " His gaze moved over her. "Looks like Holden's collecting some fringe benefits along with a paycheck."

Rachel jerked her hand away from him, then watched Tad turn on his heel and saunter away toward the parking lot. She sank down on the bench with a sick, hollow feeling in the pit of her stomach.

"It can't be true."

But then she remembered how she and Hank first met—and how easily he'd agreed to her deal. Why would a sexy veterinarian agree to fake a romance with a woman he barely knew?

But that's my job.

She closed her eyes, realizing he'd spoken those words to her only a few minutes earlier. If only she'd known he'd meant it literally.

"Hey, I saw Tad talking to you," Hank said, walking up behind her. "What was that about?"

"Nothing important." She turned to face him, suddenly feeling very tired. "I just want to go home."

On Sunday afternoon, Rachel lay on the tweed sofa in her office while Gina played therapist. She was angry and hurt and confused. Part of her understood why her friends had lied to her, but that didn't make it right.

"So tell me how you feel about Russell returning to your life," Gina asked her.

Staring up at the ceiling, Rachel saw a dead bug in the fluorescent light fixture and vaguely wondered if Russell would want it for his upcoming birthday.

Or maybe a bug zapper. A gift that kept on giving.

"How do I feel about Russell?" Rachel mused. "I'm not sure. I was angry with him at first, but maybe I'm the one at fault. Maybe I don't see things as they really are."

"That doesn't sound like you." Gina thumbed through a mercenary magazine in her search for a perfect hit man. "You're the most reality-based person I know."

"Yes, that's how every girl wants to be described. *She's reality-based and has a great sense of humor*."

Gina peered at Rachel over the top of the magazine. "What's wrong with you today?"

"I think I'm having trust issues." Rachel started wondering if she should seek counseling. Maybe that would help solve the mounting problems in her life. Perhaps Dr. Craig would take her on. She'd inherited several of his patients, so he might have room for her in his caseload.

"What kind of trust issues?" Gina asked, setting the magazine aside.

She shrugged, feeling petty and too hurt to care. "I guess issues about trusting myself and my judgment. I don't think I'm a very good judge of people. For instance, I never thought Hank would invite my ex-fiancé to stay with him. Who does that?"

"Hank's a nice guy. Have you seen the website for his vet clinic? He rehabilitates injured wildlife and trains therapy dogs."

"Yes, he looks very good on paper. And in person, if I'm honest." Rachel picked up the yellow sofa pillow next to her and wrapped her arms around it. "But help me figure out why he'd offer a room in his house to a complete stranger."

Gina didn't quite meet her gaze. "I don't know? Loneliness?"

"According to Lacie, the man needs a revolving door on his house just to keep his girlfriends from bumping into each other." Rachel shook her head. "No, I find it suspicious. I think he's up to something."

Gina cleared her throat. "Rachel, listen. I have to tell you something and I don't think you're going be happy about it."

"Gee, what could it be?" She tossed the pillow aside and stood up. "Is it that my best friends hired a guy behind my back to protect me and never said one word about it?"

"Oh, no!" Gina grimaced. "How did you find you? Did Hank tell you?"

"No, Hank didn't say a word. He had no problem keeping that secret from me." She swallowed hard to keep her from trembling. "It was Tad."

"Tad?" Gina crinkled her brow. "Tad the flosser?"

"Yes, we saw him last night at the Wildcat Tavern. We almost got arrested too, but that's a story for another time."

Gina leaped from her chair and rounded the desk. "Rach, please forgive us! Molly and I have been feeling so guilty about keeping this from you. We never meant to hurt you—just the opposite. We were scared that horrible stalker was going to do something to you." Tears shimmered in her brown eyes. "We didn't know where else to turn."

Despite her disappointment, Rachel knew Gina's regret was genuine. And looking back on her own disregard of the potential danger, she could understand why they did it.

Then she blurted out the worst part. "I kissed him, Gina. Several times. It was supposed to be fake, but...I liked it. I liked it way too much."

Gina stared at her. "And that's bad?"

"Yes!" She began to pace in front of the sofa.

"Because you and Molly were *paying* him to kiss me. Maybe he hated it."

"Seriously?" Gina smiled. "You've been messed up since Russell left you. You're one of the most confident women I know, but not around men. Not anymore. I think you rejected all those blind dates before they could reject you."

She stopped pacing and sat down on the sofa. "I can't think about that right now. I have a stalker threatening to kill me."

"What are you going to do about Hank?"

Rachel sighed, feeling torn in so many directions. "I don't know yet."

"Well, he's hired through the end of the week." Gina sat down next to Rachel and draped one arm around her shoulders. "So why don't you make him earn his pay?"

The next morning, Rachel walked into her office building and down the lobby that led to the Craig Clinic, resisting the urge to look over her shoulder.

While driving to work this morning she'd noticed a white Ford Taurus in the lane behind her for a few blocks before it pulled off onto a side street. Her common sense told her there were plenty of white

Tauruses in Pine City and one of them might belong to her stalker.

But then she'd remember the last line of that creepy verse, *I'm coming for you*, and knew she had to be vigilant. But not vigilant enough to let Hank stay over the past two nights to keep watch. She'd firmly told him that she could watch out for herself and Georgie was there to warn her if there was trouble.

He'd finally agreed, but hadn't sounded happy about it. For all she knew, he'd parked outside her house last night. But the few times she'd checked, his pickup truck had been nowhere in sight.

And Georgie hadn't barked at all last evening. Instead, she'd cuddled right next to Rachel on the sofa, as if wanting to comfort her. It was difficult to stay angry at a man who had such a sweet dog. But it didn't help her feel less embarrassed by the whole situation.

She opened the door leading into the Craig Clinic and smiled at Steven who sat behind the reception desk.

"Good morning, Dr. Grant," he said, looking more solemn than usual. Then he leaned forward and whispered, "They're waiting for you in your office."

She stopped a moment and looked between him and her closed office door, a sinking feeling in her chest. Then she squared her shoulders and continued the rest of the way down the hall.

When Rachel opened the door, she saw Dr. Craig, Noah, and Jenna standing in the center of her office. They turned to face her and she could tell by their expressions that she wasn't going to like what they had to say.

"Good morning," she greeted them, hoping for the best. Walking to her desk, she set down her purse and briefcase, then laid her coat over the office chair. "This is a surprise. Did I forget a meeting?"

"No." Dr. Craig cleared his throat. "Rachel, we need to talk about your situation."

She rounded the desk to join them. "I see."

"As you have probably guessed," Dr. Craig continued, "we're here about the threat you received on live television last Thursday. And, of course, we're very concerned for you."

"I'm fine," she told them. "I'm taking precautions and still working to identity the stalker. The police have gotten involved too, after that last threat was made."

"Unfortunately," Jenna said sharply, "it's not just about you anymore." Then her tone softened. "Your stalker is obviously escalating and threatening violence. That means, as long as he's out there, we're at risk and our patients are at risk too."

She looked at all three of them. "You didn't mention any of this on Friday, the day after the interview."

Noah took a step toward her. "Not everyone watches *Pine City People*, so it took a while for the word to spread. According to Steven, some patients left messages over the weekend canceling their appointments."

"And there were more calls this morning," Jenna added, placing a hand on her pregnant belly. "And they're not just your patients canceling, it's affecting all of us."

Dr. Craig nodded. "And I've spoken with our insurer. They advised me that if we have knowledge of potential threats to people or property here, that we must take action to mitigate any possible damages in the future."

"Damages?" Rachel echoed.

"That means we could get sued," Noah said. "And even if we win, then the rates we pay go sky high."

Dr. Craig held up one hand. "Forgive us, Rachel. I know talking about money sounds crass when your life could be in danger. But we have to consider all the implications."

Rachel had never felt so helpless. And she couldn't blame them for their concerns, especially if patients were too scared to come to the clinic. "I don't know what to say."

"Everyone knows this isn't your fault," Jenna assured her. "We are very worried about you. But..."

"We've made a decision," Noah interjected, "that

it would be in the best interest of the clinic and everyone involved for you to take a leave of absence."

"Hopefully, it will be a short one," Dr. Craig added.

Rachel couldn't speak, stunned by their decision. She'd sensed something drastic was happening when she'd first walked in the office, but shutting her off from her practice and from her patients hadn't even entered her mind.

"You can't do that," she said at last.

"We can," Noah countered. "According to the partnership agreement we all signed, the majority rules on matters of safety for patients and staff."

"And the vote was unanimous," Jenna informed her.

Dr. Craig walked over to Rachel and gently patted her shoulder. "It's not forever, Rachel. Just until this man stalking you is caught and contained."

"And if he's never caught?" Rachel asked, already knowing the answer. She'd be unemployable at the Craig Clinic or any other practice in Pine City. His threats could go on forever, like a ticking time bomb that never goes off.

"We'll cross that bridge when we come to it," Jenna told her. "We're worried about your safety, but ours as well, and the patients. I'm sorry it's come to this."

"So am I," Noah agreed as he and Jenna walked toward the door. "We all hope it's resolved soon."

When just Rachel and Dr. Craig were left in her office, she turned to him. "What about virtual therapy? I could continue to treat my patients from my computer at home."

He sighed. "I'm sure many of your patients would agree to that type of therapy, but I believe it's still a risk. If your stalker ever learned the identities of the patients still in contact with you, they could be in danger. I know the chance of that is probably slim."

Rachel nodded as the gravity of the situation was starting to sink. "But if even one of them was threatened or harmed, I could never forgive myself."

"Just think of this as putting your career on pause. Between the three of us, we can handle your patient load until you come back." He looked around office. "Are all of your patient files here?"

"No," she said, feeling a little numb. "I took several files home with me to catch up on paperwork. I'll finish those up today and bring them back to you tomorrow."

"That sounds good." He sighed as he turned to leave. "Again, I'm very sorry."

When she was finally alone, Rachel looked around her office. All she'd wanted was her own practice in Pine City. She thought about all the work she'd done to build her clientele and all the people she'd helped.

And now it was all slipping through her fingers because of some letters and a creepy phone call.

"No," she said softly. "I won't sit by and let it happen." She walked over to her desk and retrieved her cell phone from her purse to call Hank.

He answered on the first ring. "Rachel, are you okay?"

"Not really," she said honestly. "We need to talk."

❧ 12 ❧

Later that afternoon, Rachel arrived at Hank's house. She'd left home early for their meeting, allowing herself plenty of time to find his country acreage. But the directions he'd given her were perfect, so she'd arrived about twenty minutes early.

As she turned her car onto his long gravel driveway and drove toward his house, her breath caught in her throat. Hank's place was like a small paradise. The house and small red barn were the only buildings she could see for miles and had been built near a small pristine lake surrounded by tall cottonwood trees.

Horses grazed peacefully in a meadow across the road from his house, while cows and a few small calves populated a lush pasture just behind it.

She parked her car on the paved driveway in front of the modern two-story home made of brick and stone. From her perspective, it looked big enough to house a large family, which she found an interesting choice for a single man who claimed to love bachelor life.

Then she took a deep breath, reminding herself that this was business only. Because that had been Hank's perspective from the beginning. "You can do this," she said aloud as she switched off the ignition and climbed out of her car.

It had been her idea to meet here after Hank has offered to come to her place to talk. But she feared he'd try to convince her to let him stay overnight again, just for her protection.

But the truth was that she wanted to see where and how he lived. She'd formed an idea in her mind about him that night in the diner that he was this altruistic good guy who had only wanted to help her out.

But now she knew the truth—that he'd been doing it for the money. And that fact hurt some place deep inside of her.

Rachel shook it off as she reached the front door and rang the doorbell. She could face anything if it meant finding her stalker soon and getting her life back.

The door opened and Russell stood on the other side.

Rachel blinked in surprise at her ex-fiancé. He wore a gray pin-striped suit that looked similar to the one Hank had worn on the television show.

The jacket hung a little loosely on Russell's shoulders, but went well with the blue silk tie and the white oxford shirt. He looked like a new man. He'd shaved, revealing that deep cleft in his chin she'd always loved. And he'd also gotten his hair cut.

Russell, her one-time Prince Charming, looked the part today compared to the scruffy traveler who had shown up on her doorstep only a few days ago.

"Hi, Rachel," Russell said with a smile. "You look amazing."

"Thanks." She peered into the living room. "I'm here to see Hank. Is he around?"

"No, he left a while ago on some vet emergency. But he should be back soon if you want to come in."

She hesitated for a moment, then nodded. "Okay, sure."

It was strange being alone with Russell in Hank's home. She looked around, finding an odd juxtaposition of country-style décor and remnants of bachelor life. Something told her Grandma Hattie might have had a hand in helping him decorate.

The living room looked cozy, with a gray leather sofa and two matching oversized recliners. A blue-

and-white farmhouse-style rug covered a good portion of the hardwood floor and a giant television hung on the wall.

"This is perfect timing," Russell said as they moved into the living room. "The two of us getting together like this."

"The two of us?" Rachel echoed, taking a seat on the sofa and wondering if Russell had gotten the wrong impression. "Hank invited me here after I called him this morning. I didn't even know you'd be here."

"I have been busy going on job interviews." He sat down in the nearest recliner. "Hence the suit."

"Oh, that's good. What kind of job are you looking for?"

"Something in my field, of course." He shook his head. "There still aren't many jobs for entomologists in Pine City."

She nodded, remembering the disagreements they used to have about his job options. He'd wanted her to relocate with him so he could find a job he loved.

But Rachel had just started her practice and been building her clientele. And she'd witnessed Russell starting and then quitting too many 'jobs he loved' to risk her career.

"I'm so glad you're here." Russell leaned forward in the recliner, his gaze intense on her. "Hank knows how much I've been wanting to talk to you alone. Maybe this was his way of making it happen."

A prickle of uneasiness shot through her. She was almost certain Hank hadn't invited her to his home as a way of playing matchmaker. He didn't act like he even liked Russell, much less wanted them to get back together. But she'd learned the hard way that Hank was a very good actor.

"I hope you're hungry," Russell said. "When I heard saw your car in the driveway, I popped something in the oven for us to snack on."

"You didn't have to make anything for me." Then she smiled. "And since when did you take up cooking?"

"Most of the great chefs of the world are men, so I think I can handle a little snack. After all, I do have a college degree."

She didn't need a college degree to smell something burning. A smoke alarm went off somewhere, the shrill warning signal echoing throughout the big house.

Russell got up and walked over to Rachel, clasping her hands in his. They felt warm and callused. The hands of a man who had handled hundreds of insects. "I'm so glad you're here, Rach," he said over the piercing wail of the smoke alarm. "It feels just like old times."

After he left the room, Rachel had a sudden urge

to run out the door and take off. How could she tell Russell she had no interest in rekindling their romance? Especially when he looked so hopeful, so handsome, and so happy to see her?

When he'd first shown up on her doorstep last Friday night, she'd been too shocked to assess her true feelings. Then she'd learned the truth about Hank being hired to protect her and began to doubt her own perceptions.

She still liked Russell and admired his dedication to his profession. And she still remembered the physical attraction they'd had for each other. But after that first sizzling kiss with Hank, she knew a mere flicker wasn't enough for her anymore. Russell Baker had been her first love, but not the kind of love that lasted. At least not for her. Now she was even grateful that he'd taken off last February, before they'd both made a dreadful mistake.

What a difference a year makes. Or maybe it was the different man that had changed everything for her. Hank might just be doing his job, but she couldn't deny her feelings for him.

Russell returned to the living room with a tray containing two glasses of wine and a platter.

"Here we go, a merlot for my lady," he said, setting the tray on the coffee table between them, then handing her a glass. Then he held out the platter to her. "Hors d'oeuvres?"

She looked at the tiny pizza triangle that had obviously been cut from a frozen pizza. "Thank you," she said, taking it from him and nibbling on an unburnt corner.

Then he sat down and cleared his throat. "The truth is...I want you back. I know it's been a bumpy road for us, but I'm sure we've learned things along the way. And one thing that I've learned is that you're the perfect woman for me."

She looked up into his brown eyes, not wanting to hurt him despite the way he'd abandoned her. But the words stuck in her throat. Maybe she'd wait until after he finished the frozen pizza appetizers. In her experience, men usually seemed to handle bad news better on a full stomach.

"I'd like to propose a toast," Russell said, holding up his wineglass. "To the *Rachelona cyanella,* the most beautiful beetle on earth, named for the most beautiful woman on earth."

She took a sip of wine, dismally seeing her future stretched out before her if she settled for Russell. Instead of having children, she'd be godmother to a beetle. Somehow, that wasn't enough for her. So now the question was how to let him down easy.

"Russell," she began.

"No." He rushed over to her, taking a seat on the sofa next to her and reaching for her hand. "Don't say it, because you know we were always meant to be together."

"Am I interrupting?" Hank asked, standing just inside the front door.

She choked on her wine, coughing as Russell stood up to face him. "Rachel and I need a little privacy, if you don't mind."

"No," Rachel gasped, rising to her feet and still coughing. "Russell, I'm sorry, but I really need to talk to Hank. Do you mind if we finish our conversation later?"

Russell's mouth pressed into a firm line as he looked between the two of them, then he gave a sharp nod. "Fine. I have errands to run anyway. But we will talk, Rachel."

It was a declaration, not a question, so she didn't respond as he turned and walked out the front door.

Hank closed the door behind him, then slowly turned to face her. "What was all that about?"

"A misunderstanding." She cleared her throat, then looked him straight in the eye. "Just like you and I have had a misunderstanding. Because I know you've been lying to me."

Completely at a loss for words, Hank stared at her. Just a moment ago, he'd heard Russell trying to win Rachel back. And now, she was calling Hank a liar.

And she was right. A lie of omission, but a lie all the same. And made all the worse because of everything that had happened between them. "Rachel, I..."

She held up her hand to stop him. "It doesn't matter now. Gina told me all about Cowboy Confidential, and I guess this gig was some kind of fun vacation for you. But the important thing is that I still need some hired help and you're on the payroll until the end of the week, right?"

"Right." In that moment, he saw something in Rachel that had always been there but he hadn't recognized until now. Anger at him, to be sure. But she had an inner strength, a belief in herself and her convictions, that made her truly special.

Plus one of the best headbutts he'd ever witnessed. She was amazing. And torn between working with him or killing him, judging by the fiery sparks in her green eyes.

"What do you need from me?" he asked her.

"We've got to come up with a short list of the most possible suspects. My career is at stake now. And it's not just about me, my patients and co-workers could be in danger too. I've been put on a leave of absence until my stalker is caught. So it's either catch him soon or..."

He heard the catch in her throat and saw the way she was trying to hold it all together. "Or what?"

"Or I leave Pine City to start over somewhere else. And just hope he doesn't follow me there."

He hated that it had come to this and that he was part of the pain he heard in her voice. Maybe he'd actually made things worse for her, because they sure hadn't made any progress in identifying her stalker.

But he wasn't about to stop looking, no matter how long it took. He owed her that much after letting her down on Saturday night. She'd been right by his side one moment, and the next moment Tad had grabbed her.

One hand curled into a fist just thinking about it. The one time she'd truly been in physical danger, he'd turned his back at just the wrong moment. They'd been lucky it was just that drunk loser instead of her stalker.

But he couldn't let it happen again. "So, let's think about this," he began. "You're put on a leave of absence. Your patients and work colleagues might be at risk. And the only way out of this situation might be you leaving town and starting over somewhere else."

She looked thoughtful and slowly nodded. "Maybe I've been all wrong about him. He doesn't want me. He just wants me to go away."

"I think you're right. He sent those letters and

made that one phone call, but otherwise, he's kept his distance."

"Like he's trying to scare me away." She shook her head in disbelief. "We thought we'd flush him out with jealousy when he saw us together. That he wanted to be close to me. But what if it's just the opposite?"

Brainy and beautiful, he thought to himself. The perfect combination.

"You think he wants you to go away?" Hank asked, following her line of thought. "To leave Pine City. Maybe even Texas?"

She nodded. "It makes the most sense when I think about it. But *why* does he want to drive me away?"

Hank was silent, pondering that very question. At last he said, "Let's think who would benefit if you left town. How about that neighbor of yours? What's his name? Newt? The one who keeps pestering you to buy you out."

She nodded. "Yes, Newt Beaufort. He's been a real pain, but I haven't heard anything from him for the past couple of weeks."

"Isn't that when the stalker started ramping up?"

"Yes, it is." She reached into her purse and pulled out a notepad and pen. "Okay, so I'm going to put Newt on the short list."

"Who else can we put there?"

She shook her head. "I hate to even say it, much less think it. But my colleagues at the Craig Clinic didn't waste much time putting me on leave. And they're going to split all my patients between them."

"Is there one therapist in particular that you have doubts about?"

"No, not really. I mean Noah Lopez has a made of couple of snide comments about my heavy patient load. And Jenna Rifkin has expressed worry that some of her patients will just move to the other female therapist in the practice while she's on maternity leave."

"So there is some professional jealousy?"

She shrugged. "I don't know if it's jealousy as much as competition. But I can't imagine any of them threatening to kill me on live television."

"The voice on that call was disguised," he reminded her. "I think that increases the chance it's someone you know. So who else can we add to the list?" He was waiting for her to name the most obvious person, not wanting to do it himself.

"I could always add my parents and brother?" she said wryly. "They've been wanting me to move home almost since the day I left." She put her head in her hands. "And maybe that is the simplest solution."

"Is that what you want?" he asked sincerely.

She met his gaze, then shook her head. "No. I want to stay right here and find this guy. If he'll do this to me, who knows what he might do when someone else gets in his way."

"Good," Hank said. "I'm going to check in with Luke and see if they've made any progress identifying that caller. He said it would be a long shot, but maybe he's got something by now."

"There's one thing we're forgetting," Rachel said, "and it puts a hole in my theory that the stalker is trying to drive me away."

"What's that?"

"The red Buick," she told him. "That doesn't fit with the notion that he wants to keep his distance and just stalk me from afar. You saw him drive by my house twice and even got his license plate number. And you could have caught him during that chase."

"I didn't forget about the red Buick." He hesitated for a moment, but then decided he'd never lie or keep things from her again. "There's something I need to show you."

Rachel walked into his home office, a cozy room on the first floor of the house and sat in a chair next to him at the desk, watching as he opened up his laptop and the screen lit up. A few clicks later and a large, yellow insect filled the computer scene.

"Ugh!" Rachel reared back in her chair. "That's the last thing I want to see!"

"There's about twenty-five more photos like that on here. And they all belong to Russell. He showed them to me last night and I learned more about insects in North Texas than I ever wanted to know."

She looked away from the screen. "Yes, I assumed the pictures belonged to Russell. But why are they on your computer and what do they have to do with my stalker? You don't think Russell..." Rachel looked down on her list and realized the most obvious name was missing. He'd wanted her to go to Africa with him before he'd left her. She'd refused because she was building her own career and didn't want to leave her patients.

But could the man she'd once loved—or had thought she loved—be the same one who had recited, *Roses are red, corpses are blue. Keep watch, my love. I'm coming for you?* It was too awful to consider.

"Hold on, I'm getting there," he said, scrolling through more bug photos. Then he stopped and pointed to a picture of an insect that looked about five inches long draped across part of a rusty bucket. "According to the description Russell wrote, that is a Texas giant redheaded centipede."

Rachel shuddered. "That thing is huge, but why are we looking at it?"

"Do you see the name on the bucket?"

Rachel leaned closer, lightly brushing against his shoulder for a better look. There was something printed on the rim of the bucket in black marker. "Does that say...Sassy?"

"Yes. And I recognize that bucket. I saw it when Lee showed me what she was feeding her mule. There were a couple of buckets like that with Sassy's name written on them."

"Okay," Rachel said slowly, her mind whirling. "Putting aside why anyone would put a mule's name on a bucket, what does this mean?"

He swirled in his office chair to face her. "This centipede photo was taken three weeks ago, according to the date recorded on it. That means Russell was in Pine City three weeks ago."

Rachel sat back in her chair. "So he didn't just fly in from Africa on the day he showed up at my house. He was here before I found that note in my pocket?" Her gaze met his. "And he was there during the time Lee's red Buick was stolen?"

"Yes to all of that." Hank reached out to touch her hand, then hesitated and pulled back again. "Do you think it's possible he could have slipped that note in your coat pocket at Bonnie's Diner without you seeing him?"

"I'm sure he could have. I barely recognized him when he showed up on my doorstep last Friday. He was scruffy and looked so...different." She forced a smile, even as the shock still reverberated through her. "And when I eat pancakes at the diner, I rarely look up from my plate, so a human-sized redheaded centipede could walk by me and I'd be oblivious."

That made him smile. "So what do you want to do now?"

She shook her head. "I can't believe the Russell I knew, the man I planned to marry, could ever do something like this. Although, as a therapist I know people are complex and can lose themselves when under enormous stress."

"Or he could just be a jerk," Hank said bluntly. "Like you said, people are complex, so maybe he's hidden that part of himself from you until now."

"That doesn't say much about my skills for reading people."

"He wasn't your patient," Hank reminded her. "You loved him."

Rachel rose out of the chair. "Did I? I'm not so sure anymore. These past few weeks..." Then she stopped herself from saying something that would make her look even more pathetic. "We have to confront him and find out the truth."

Hank stood up and walked over to her. "I agree. But let me go talk to Lee Demby first and find out what she knows. That could give us some insight about his motives—if he is your..."

"Stalker?" she finished for him. Then she walked

quickly over to the sofa and swept up her purse as she made her way to the front door, determined to be as far away from Hank as possible before she lost it.

"Rachel, please wait," Hank called after her.

But she ignored him, closing door behind her and making a run for her car.

❧ 13 ❧

That evening, Rachel met with her Lonely Hearts group at her office, defying her partners for one last meeting of the group that meant so much to her. So much had happened since their meeting last week that it seemed like a lifetime ago.

"Well, I did it," Frank announced. "I finally found a woman who loves bass fishing even more than I do." He grinned as reached into his paper sack of homemade caramel corn Edith had brought for everyone. She'd even added a cut-out pink heart to each sack with the words, '*You don't have to be in love to be happy*' written on it.

"Loves fishing more than you, Frank?" Lacie said, laughing. "That's hard to believe. Where did you meet her?"

"At a new bait shop near Callahan's Lake." His grin widened. "She's the owner."

Edith turned to him. "Does that mean you might get free worms for the rest of your life?"

"Fish bait isn't just about worms anymore," he said, turning more serious. "There's plenty of good bait science out there. It all depends on the type of fish, the time of year, and the water environment to determine the best types of bait to use. Now take the wide-mouth bass..."

Everyone groaned at his fish lecture. "Sorry, Frank," Rachel told him, "but I'm afraid you're outnumbered."

Frank chuckled. "Too bad Hank's not here. He's someone who would appreciate talking about bait."

"Where is he, anyway?" Lacie asked Rachel, a knowing twinkle in her eyes. "And are you excited for your Valentine's Day date with Hank at Rawling's Steakhouse tomorrow night?"

"We all saw you two on Midge's show," Edith told Rachel. "As soon as I heard from Midge that you'd be on, I called everyone in the group."

"I'm not sure what the plans are yet," Rachel hedged. In truth, she'd forgotten about their date. Valentine's Day was the last thing on her mind.

"Well, I hope our boycott isn't giving you pause," Edith told her. "It's been a fun way to approach the holiday this year, but it's also reminded me it's time to take some risks." She set her popcorn sack in her lap, her brown eyes gleaming with excitement. "You've told us that taking risks is part of life. That's why Frank and I and his new lady friend are busy getting ready for our trip."

"Trip?" Gina echoed.

"That's right," Frank affirmed with a chuckle. "Edith talked me into going on a cruise. Peg, the owner of the bait shop, is going too. She loves bait science as much as I do, and we're going to try some deep-sea fishing."

Rachel was delighted for them. "All three of you are going on this cruise? That's wonderful!"

"Yep," Frank replied, winking at Edith. "It's a singles cruise for people over fifty-five. We thought it might be nice to meet some new blood."

"Good for you!" Rachel couldn't believe this was the same quiet, recalcitrant man who'd been strong-armed by his daughter into joining the Lonely Hearts group. "I'm so proud of you, Frank. And you too, Edith."

Edith breathed a happy sigh. "I can't live in the past anymore— and my husband would be the first one to tell me so." She clapped her hands together. "I haven't been so excited about anything in years! I'm finally making *myself* happy instead of waiting for someone else to do it."

"Me, too," Lacie announced. "I'm not going on a

cruise, but I decided that I'm through waiting around for my boyfriend to come back to me. In fact, I don't even want him anymore. I'm going back to college, and I'm going to start a new job teaching ballet to beginners. It doesn't pay as much as my waitress job, but I can't think of anything that would make me happier."

"I'm so proud of you, Lacie!" Rachel exclaimed, suddenly realizing her group didn't really need her anymore. They were branching out and seeking new adventures.

But what would she do without them?

"We owe it all to you, Dr. Grant," Edith chimed in. "This Valentine's Day boycott worked for me in a way I never imagined. Instead of waiting for someone to make me their Valentine, I'm going to start looking for someone good enough to be mine."

"So am I," Gina announced. "Once this anger toward my soon-to-be ex-husband has passed. I'm still in the rage phase and I wouldn't be good for anyone right now. But I can finally glimpse a happier future. It's just going to take me a while to get there."

"And what about you, Dr. Grant?" Lacie rolled up her empty popcorn sack. "If you're hot for the veterinarian, I think you should go for it."

Rachel blushed, then glanced over at Gina. "It's...complicated."

"Or maybe it's fate," Gina countered. 'It all depends on your state of mind."

"Whoa," Lacie said, laughing. "Turning Dr. Grant's words back on her. I like it! But she also says you don't need to be in love to be happy."

"But it's a fun place to start," Frank added.

Everyone laughed, then Gina said, "I know I'm the newest member, but I'm going to miss all of you."

"Just because the group is breaking up doesn't mean we can't get together on our own," Lacie told her. "We can all meet for coffee somewhere, same day and time, just a different place."

"Sure we can." Edith turned to Rachel. "Would you join us too?"

"I'll plan on it," Rachel promised. "As soon as the time is right." She didn't have to say more because they understood, and then Gina changed the subject.

They chatted for another hour or so before the members slowly trickled out until only Gina and Rachel were left.

"You were quieter than usual tonight," Rachel said. "Are you all right?"

"No, I'm really not." Gina sat on the sofa, her head down as she tore little strips of paper from the top of her popcorn sack. Then she looked at Rachel, seated in the armchair across from her. "Because I think I ruined my best friend's chance of happiness. I know you're in love with Hank. I see it on your face whenever you say his name."

"Oh, don't tell me I'm that transparent." Rachel leaned forward, her head in her hands. "And I'm not sure know how I feel about him. He lied to me and..."

"He lied by omission and only because Molly and I demanded that he not say anything to you about this job. Because we knew you'd fire him on the spot."

"And you were right. But it turns out I did need him. Because I saw him today and I think he may have found a lead to identifying my stalker."

Gina tossed the sack aside. "And you're just telling me this now! Who is it?"

She sucked in a deep breath. "We think it's Russell."

"Your Russell?"

Rachel nodded. "Crazy, right? I really know how to pick 'em." Then she found herself smiling. "It turns out, you and Molly have great instincts. Neither of you liked him from the start. I'm the one with the advanced psychology degree, but you're the ones who sensed something was off with him."

"That's why they say love is blind."

Rachel swallowed hard as tears burned her eyes. "I thought I loved Russell until I met Hank. Maybe I still don't know what love is, because I read him wrong too. He was just doing his job."

"You don't know that until you ask him," Gina said gently. "Or at least go on that date with him tomorrow night. Just the two of you, with no secrets and no agenda. See what happens."

Rachel was so tempted, but she shook off the idea. "I can't do anything until I know this crazy stalker nonsense is in my past. I can't even do the work I love." She took a deep shuddering breath. "And Hank hasn't said a word about that Valentine's date, so I don't think he's planning on it either."

Gina stood up and walked over to her. "Do you know how much I want to shake some sense into you right now? And this is coming from a person who has multiple detailed plans on the best way to kill her husband."

Rachel laughed, despite her heartache. "How about giving me a hug instead," she told her friend, rising to her feet and wrapping her arms around Gina. "And please burn those murder plans before someone finds them. It's time to move forward."

Gina hugged her back. "I'll move forward if you will."

"You've got a deal."

On Tuesday afternoon, Hank sat parked on the side of the road across from Lee Demby's cabin. He'd learned the hard way not to enter her property without her permission. But he'd been staked out there for most of the day, as well as the evening before, waiting for her to make an appearance. He couldn't imagine what had kept Lee away from home for so long and he wasn't planning to ask.

At least Sassy was there. From his vantage point, he could see the mule inside the fenced area that led into the barn. He leaned back against the headrest as a Patsy Cline song played on the radio. He missed the vet clinic and the trips to neighboring farms and ranches. He missed Grandma Hattie's honey buns which had run out four days ago.

And he really missed Rachel. He might not be able to fall in love, but he couldn't stop thinking about her. And that was new for him. While he waited, he sent her a text about their Valentine's Day dinner schedule for tonight: *See you at seven?*

A loud rumble caught his attention and he saw an old Chevy truck rumbling up the road toward him. Lee sat in the driver's seat, the top of her head barely visible above the large steering wheel. She gunned the truck as she passed Hank on the road, then swung it into her driveway, the tires spitting gravel in every direction.

A text dinged on his phone and he smiled when he saw Rachel's reply: *Yes.* Their date was on—he might still have a chance with her.

He waited a few minutes for Lee to park her truck. Then he climbed out of the cab of his pickup, hoping she didn't have her shotgun handy.

"Hey, Lee," he called out, his hands raised in the air as he walked onto her gravel driveway. "You got a minute?"

Lee stood next to her truck wearing a pair of faded overalls and a brown flannel shirt. She swung the truck door closed, but it bounced open again.

Muttering under her breath, she raised one skinny leg and kicked the door shut with her booted foot. "Back to see Sassy? She has that effect on people. They all love her just as much as I do."

"How is Sassy?" he asked, lowering his hands.

Lee glanced over at the mule. "Better than before. Seems more cheerful too." Then she looked at Hank. "Can't say the same for you."

"I'm hoping you can help with that."

Lee snorted. "I'm not the cheerful type, so you might want to look elsewhere."

"How about a barter then?" he said, walking toward her. "You answer a few of my questions, and I'll provide free veterinary care for Sassy for the rest of her life."

Lee scowled. "Depends on the questions. Spit 'em out and then I'll decide if it's worth it to me."

He knew going in it wouldn't be easy. "I'm going to show you a photo of a large insect," he said, slowly removing the picture from the pocket in his jacket. He unfolded it and handed it to her. "Sassy's bucket is in the background, which tells me the photo was taken here. Do you know anything about it?"

Lee took it from him. "Maybe. Who wants to know?"

"Rachel. You remember her?"

A smile softened Lee's brusqueness. "Oh, you mean that pretty redhead you couldn't stop staring it. Yeah, I remember her. Seem to recall she left you in the dust after you made me drag her out here."

"You're the one who called her," he began, then pulled back. Arguing with Lee wouldn't get anywhere. Better to be blunt. "Rachel's in trouble and the photographer of this insect is the reason for it."

"So he put a bun in her oven?"

Hank's mouth fell open. "No! The guy might be a nutcase and she's in danger."

"Simmer down," Lee told him. "I don't know what goes on in you folks' private lives. All I know is a guy name Russ took this picture and lots more to boot. He'd heard about the infestation at my place from somebody in town, I guess. Seems that kind of critter is usually found in Texas Hill Country."

"How long was Russell here?"

Lee considered the question. "About three to four days, but I made him sleep in the barn. He was the first one to let me know about Sassy's digestive problems." Then she stood a little taller. "And he said my place was one of the best breeding grounds for bugs he'd ever seen."

"And when was this?"

"Maybe three or four weeks ago. 'Bout the time Sassy started having that gas trouble."

Now that Lee had confirmed it, he only had a couple more questions. "And that was before your car was stolen?"

"Sure was." She reached to scratch her grizzled cheek. "You think Russ took it?"

Hank nodded, wondering just how long Russell had been in Texas. "I think it's a good possibility."

"Well, if you find him, can you bring him here? As you know, I like to deal with these problems myself."

Hank smiled, liking Lee more with each passing moment. "I'll see what I can do."

Rachel walked into the Craig Clinic on Tuesday afternoon carrying her box of files. She walked up to the reception desk, where Steven sat working on a crossword puzzle.

"Hi, Steven," she greeted him, startling the young man.

He quickly closed his puzzle book. "Hi, Dr. Grant. I wasn't expecting to see you today."

She set the file box on the desk. "I promised Dr. Craig that I'd bring my patient files in today. Can you give them to him?"

He spun in his chair to look at the closed door to Dr. Craig's office. "Sure, but he's free if you'd like to take them in yourself. Then you could answer any questions he might have."

"Okay, I'll do that," she said with a smile. "Thanks."

"No problem." He got up from his chair and rounded the desk. "I'll open the door for you."

Picking up the box, Rachel followed Steven down the long hallway. She passed her own office door, the room dark through the glass panels at the top of the office walls. And it might stay that way for a long time to come.

She shook that thought out of her head and waited as Steven knocked on Dr. Craig's office door, then cracked it open. "Dr. Grant's here to see you."

"Yes, send her in, please."

Rachel squared her shoulders and walked into his office. She'd come here with a plan, hoping she could convince him that her leave of absence would be short enough that he wouldn't need to reassign her patients. "Hello, Dr. Craig."

"Dr. Grant, it's wonderful to see you." He reached for the file box. "Here, let me take that for you and please have a seat." He lifted the box out of her arms and carried it over to the small mahogany table near his desk. "I truly am sorry it's come to this."

"So am I." Rachel sat down in the armchair directly across from him.

Her gaze moved over his large bookcase, where she saw copies of the bestselling book, *The Brain Archeologist: Digging for Secrets*.

There were foreign copies of the book there too. Dr. Craig's book had been a big hit twenty years ago. He'd become something of a national expert and a frequent guest on talks shows across the country.

The fame had led to him rubbing elbows with starlets and celebrities and even power political figures. All of it documented in the framed photographs hanging on his office walls.

"Maybe I'll read your book again during my hiatus. It's what made me interested in psychology in the first place."

"Thank you." He took a seat at his desk. "That's a high compliment, especially coming from such a talented therapist. The trick to success is to never stop learning."

"I'm worried that my caseload will be too much for you and Noah, especially with Jenna going on maternity leave soon."

"Don't you worry about that," he said, waving her concern away. "Noah was here in my officer earlier today, champing at the bit to take on more patients."

"I'm hoping that won't be necessary." She glanced at the cell phone, still waiting for Hank to contact her about his visit with Lee Demby. Hopefully, she wouldn't need to rescue him again. Although, it would give her the opportunity to ask him some pointed questions under the gun.

"You were saying?" Dr. Craig prodded.

"Oh, yes. I think we may have a lead on my stalker. A friend of mine is following up on it now. There's a chance you could reinstate me this week, maybe even as soon as tomorrow."

"Really?" Dr. Craig said, his pale-blue eyes twinkling. "That is wonderful news. May I ask if it's someone you know or a stranger?"

"Someone I know, unfortunately." She sighed. "I won't say any more about it in case I'm mistaken. But it's made me rethink a lot of the decisions I've made in my life. That's why I want to reacquaint myself with your book."

"You're welcome to take a copy if you'd like. My publisher continues to send me complimentary copies each year. My agent says they're still hoping to get a second book out of me."

Her phone dinged and when she glanced down at it, she saw a text from Hank that read: *See you at seven at Rawling's?*

"I'd love a copy, thank you." She stared at the text as she spoke, her heart beating faster. "The one I have is so dog-eared and filled with yellow highlights that it's hard to read anymore."

"It's my pleasure," he said, getting up from his desk and walking over to the bookcase. He plucked from the center shelf. "Here's the most recent edition." Then he scanned the other books in his collection. "Since you're on leave, perhaps I can find another book to help you pass the time."

While he was distracted, Rachel furtively typed a response to Hank's text: *Yes*.

"Ah, here's another one you might enjoy. It was written by my cousin." He carried the books over to Rachel and handed them to her. The top book featured a photo of a dog that looked just like Georgie.

"My uncle raised German shorthaired pointers when I was a youngster, so my cousin is quite the expert on them. And there are some training tips for GSPs in there too," he told her. "You'll need them because that breed can get quite rambunctious." He chuckled. "Of course, that was my experience many decades ago. But I've always favored the look of the solid liver GSPs too. Such a regal dog."

"They're beautiful," she agreed, staring at the book cover.

He walked over to the small table and lifted the lid of her file box. "This should keep me busy for the rest of the afternoon."

Rachel was still staring at the books in her hands. Something didn't seem right. She got up from the chair and headed for the door. "I'll leave you to it then. Thank you, Dr. Craig."

"You're quite welcome," he said, carrying the file box over to his desk. "And let me know if they catch your stalker. We can't wait to have you back on staff here."

She opened the door, then turned back to face him. "I never told you I had a dog."

He looked up at her. "What?"

Walking toward him, she held up the cover of the dog book. "I never told you or anyone else at the clinic that I have a dog, much less a liver-colored GSP. So you must have seen her in my backyard. You were the one out in the alley that night when she was barking, weren't you?"

"I don't...know what you're...talking about," he stammered, perspiration dotting his forehead. "I'm sure you told us about your dog. I can ask Noah..."

The truth hit Rachel like a tidal wave. Her stalker had been a man she'd admired for years. A man who'd given her the opportunity to work in his prestigious clinic. And to learn everything he knew. Walking over to the front of his desk, she planted both hands on top of it and surreptitiously pressed the intercom button with her pinkie finger.

"You've got it all wrong," he told her, his face

flushed. "No doubt you're stressed with everything that's been happening. You've simply gotten a little paranoid." He pulled a desk drawer open and fumbled inside of it. "Perhaps some medication would help..."

Then she quoted a line she'd memorized from his book. "Guilt can create both emotional and physical manifestations. The physical signs can include perspiration, facial redness and flushed skin, avoidance of eye contact..."

"Okay, enough!" he bit out. "I might have imitated your stalker, but I'm not *the* stalker."

Her heart dropped. "I don't understand."

He waved one arm toward his bookcase. "I have one book to my name, and now my editor won't even take my calls. That book I gave you is one of many that *I* purchased to help keep the sales numbers up." He shook his head. "And ten of my patients have transferred to you since you joined my clinic. At this rate, I won't have any patients left to treat by the end of the year."

Disbelief mixed with pity for the broken man in front of her. "So you're the one who called the television station and recited that awful verse? And you put that note in my coat pocket?"

He sank down in his chair, burying his face in one hand. "Yes. And I came to your house that night and your dog scared me away." He gave her a rueful smile.

"Even after years of treating offenders, I guess I'm not a very effective stalker."

"So you didn't plan to hurt me?" she asked skeptically.

"Of course not! What kind of man do you think I am?" He stared up at her, full of indignation. "I never intended to follow through on any of those silly threats. I knew you missed your family in Philadelphia, so I thought if you got uncomfortable here, you'd just go back home."

"You just asked me what kind of man you are." Rachel stood in front of his desk, thinking of all the years she'd idolized him. "I think you're the kind of man who should retire immediately."

Then she turned to the intercom box on his desk. "Did you get all that, Steven?"

"I got it, Dr. Grant."

14

By the time Hank returned from Lee's house, he barely had time to get dressed and shaved before his date with Rachel. He couldn't wait to see her again, even if it meant revealing that her ex-fiancé had been lying to her.

Lee had been helpful in confirming that Russell had been in Pine City longer than he'd claimed, but there was still no proof that he was Rachel's stalker.

He stood in front of the mirror in the upstairs bathroom, running an electric razor over the thick stubble of whiskers on his face. A splash of aftershave and he'd be out the door.

"Hey, Hank," Russell called from down the hall. "Do you have a minute?"

Hank clenched his jaw. He didn't have time to deal with Russell, although he was eager to get the truth out of him. After a quick look in the mirror, he grabbed his suit coat on his way out of his bedroom and headed down the hall to Russell's room.

"I don't have a lot of time," Hank said, standing in the open doorway of the guest room. "What do you need?"

"I packed my knapsack and I'm headed out. I just wanted to thank you for everything." Then Russell shot out one arm and hit Hank in the gut with something.

Every muscle in Hank's body instantly turned to jelly and he fell to the floor, unable to move. It felt like a thousand bees stinging at the same time.

Russell stood over him, holding a taser in his hand. "Thanks for the hospitality, but I need to be on my way now."

Hank's grew woozy and he couldn't make himself move, but it felt like he was sliding on the floor. From far away he heard the sound of Russell's voice. "I know I don't deserve her, Hank. But I won't let my Lovebug get squashed by a heel like you."

Rachel sat alone at the best table in Rawling's Steakhouse, surrounded by loving couples celebrating Valentine's Day. There was a beautiful bouquet in the center of the table, with a banner that read: *Pine City People's Most Romantic Couple*.

And Midge had spared no expense to showcase the couple that had won this dinner on her talk show.

Rachel's mouth hurt from smiling, but she didn't know how else to hide her growing uneasiness. He was late. Only five minutes late, but the patrons in the crowded restaurant were already starting to whisper. She glimpsed Gina and Molly sharing a table in the corner. They had wanted a sneak peek at their first official date. But now they were trying very hard not to look worried.

At least they weren't worried about her stalker anymore. Rachel had quickly filled them in about Dr. Craig and his downfall. The police had even called her earlier to confirm that he'd turned himself in.

Rachel ordered a glass of wine from the waiter, then sat back in her chair, her gaze riveted on the door. There was only one man she was worried about now. Any moment now, she'd see him walk in. And he'd have a wonderful excuse for running late. Maybe he'd run into traffic on Valentine's Day. Or been called out to treat a sick animal. Maybe he couldn't decide what to wear.

Seven fifteen passed and still no sign of Hank.

A reporter from Midge's paper lost interest early and began to flirt with a muscle-bound waiter. A photographer made a call on his cell phone. And the violinist Midge had hired to serenade the couple had bellied up to the bar.

By seven twenty-five Rachel had memorized the entire menu. She'd give Hank five more minutes, then order the bottomless bowl of chicken soup so she could drown herself in it. As the seconds slowly ticked by, she decided not to wait any longer. Not with everyone staring so pitifully at her. With a fake smile to all the people watching her, she pushed back her chair and headed for the ladies' restroom. Gina and Molly followed close on her heels.

"I can't believe he stood you up!" Gina exclaimed after the swinging door closed behind them with a swoosh.

"Me, neither." Rachel checked under all the stalls in case anyone lurked inside, but they were empty. Then she turned on the heel of her Italian suede pumps. "Now what am I going to do? I can't go back out there and pretend nothing is wrong."

Molly held out both hands. "Just stay calm. This is a small crisis. We can handle it."

"This a disaster," Rachel exclaimed, pacing back and forth. "I never should have agreed to meet him here tonight. Why did he even send me that text if he was going to be a no-show?"

"Maybe there's a good reason," Gina said. "It doesn't seem like something he'd do."

"How do we know that?" Molly asked her.

"Thanks to us, he only showed up in Rachel's life less than two weeks ago. We don't know anything about him, except that he does side work for Cowboy Confidential and it's got rave reviews."

Gina shook her head, her mouth pressed into a thin, angry line. "You were right about Hank all along, Rachel. The only reason he was romancing you was to help catch your stalker. But I can't believe he'd have the nerve to embarrass you in public like this. That doesn't seem like the guy who shared his deepest secret in our Lonely Hearts group."

"The same guy Lacie said had a different woman every weekend?" Rachel put a hand to her head, not wanting to believe it. Because her heart was telling her that Hank did have feelings for her.

"Face it, Rach, the guy is a rat." Molly narrowed her eyes. "And do you know what we do when we come across a rat?"

"Scream and put the house up for sale?" Gina ventured.

"No, we exterminate them," Molly said, slashing her hand in the air. "Exterminate him from your life. Don't think about him, call him, text him, or contact him in any way. You'll save yourself a lot of pain."

"I'm not ready to exterminate him yet." Rachel closed her eyes. "But I can't go back out there. What am I going to do?"

"Stay in here until the restaurant closes?" Gina suggested. "I have a deck of cards in my purse."

"No, I've got an even better idea." Rachel kicked off her shoes. "I'm going out the window."

"Rachel, no!" Molly exclaimed, grabbing her by the arm. "I won't let you throw your life away. Especially over a jerk like Hank Holden."

"Relax," Rachel said, "we're on the first floor this time. I'm only going out the window to avoid that crowd in there. I'm already the subject of gossip because of my stalker."

"What about Hank?" Gina asked.

"I'm going to track down Hank Holden and tell him exactly what I think of him."

"He's really not worth the effort," Molly warned. "I know you're the shrink, but please just take my advice and try to forget about him."

"I can't do that." Rachel reached up to unlatch the window. "When Russell left me last year, I just let him go. I never tried to find him or contact him. I never demanded any answers. Instead, I blamed myself for months, trying to figure out why he didn't want me anymore. I'm not going through that again."

"But you were engaged to Russell," Gina countered. "He owed you answers. Hank is a different story. You two barely know each other."

"Gina's right," Molly said. "Hank never should have humiliated you in public this way, but just think how much more embarrassed you'll be if you go chasing after him."

Rachel considered their arguments. It would be so easy to give up. To go home with some of her pride still intact. But her heart wouldn't let her surrender so easily. She'd known him less than two weeks, but he'd already found a place in her heart.

"Look, I can handle rejection." Rachel looked from Gina to Molly. "But I can't handle not knowing the truth. I need to find out if any of it was real."

Molly shook her head and Gina looked even more homicidal than usual.

"Don't worry," Rachel assured them as she swung one leg over the windowsill. "I'll be fine. Just try to distract that reporter until I make my getaway."

She dropped down onto a patch of thick grass outside of the restaurant. Shivers coursed through her as Gina passed her shoes through the open window. But they were shivers of anticipation. She couldn't wait until she got her hands on him.

Rachel walked barefoot through the crowded parking lot until she reached her car. Then she slung on her heels. "Ready or not, Hank. Here I come."

Hank opened his eyes, wincing at the bright, bare light bulb shining above him. He blinked twice, his head still foggy. A faint hint of mothballs mingled with the musty odor invading his nostrils. He sat up on his elbows and looked around.

He was in a closet.

It was actually a small dressing room that he'd converted into a walk-in storage closet. The light bulb illuminated the shelves lining the walls, piled full of boxes. He lay on the dusty wood floor, wondering how he got in here. Then he remembered Russell and his taser. His head swam again for a moment, then cleared.

He had a date with Rachel tonight.

He swore under his breath as he checked his watch, then lunged for the door. It was locked. Frowning at it, he tried to make sense of the situation. Why was he locked in the closet? How did he even get in here? And where was Russell? Hank pounded on the solid oak door with his fist. "Russell, are you out there? The door's locked. I've got to get out of here right now."

"Give it up, Holden," Russell called from the other side of the door. "I'm not letting you out."

"What are you talking about?" Hank shouted. "Open this door before I break it down."

"No way. I locked you in there to keep you away from Rachel. So you might as well get comfortable. You're not going anywhere for a while."

Hank gave the door a vicious kick, barely making

a dent in the wood but almost breaking his big toe. He hopped around inside the closet, gritting his teeth at the pain. Breaking down the door was not an option. He'd have to use his brains instead.

"Listen, Russ, just open the door and we can talk this out. I know you're upset about losing Rachel."

"You don't know anything, Holden," Russell said. "Rachel Grant is the most decent woman I've ever known. And she makes a lot of money. I won't let her be hurt by a user like you."

"Hey, I'm not the one that left her for a dung beetle," Hank shouted, his temper overcoming his better judgment. "Why didn't you just stay lost, Baker, instead of coming back here to stir up trouble?"

"It's a good thing I did come back," Russell countered. "To save Rachel from making the biggest mistake of her life."

"You were the biggest mistake of her life. You hurt her once, and now you're determined to hurt her again. How do you think she'll feel when I don't show up on our date tonight?"

"Relieved," Russell exclaimed, "once I explain the reason."

"You're planning to tell her you kidnapped me? It will be hard to explain that to her from a jail cell. Think it over, Baker, you're a smart man. And kidnapping is a crime."

"This isn't kidnapping," Russell said, not sounding at all worried at the prospect of studying insects behind bars. "You fainted in the closet, the door accidentally locked you in and I'm looking for the key. Don't worry, I should find it in a couple hours."

Hank resisted the urge to kick the door again. A couple of hours? So much for his date with Rachel. He didn't even want to imagine her sitting at the restaurant. Alone. Waiting for him.

She already had doubts about his sincerity, thinking he'd only kissed her and spent time with her because he'd been paid to do it. What she didn't realize is that he'd donated that money to a local rescue the day he first met her.

But now it would be his word against Russell's, and getting kidnapped by an entomologist sounded even more unbelievable than getting lost in the African bush.

"You might as well get comfortable," Russell said. "There's a thermos of coffee in there on the floor and a couple of entertaining entomology textbooks. You never know when that kind of information will come in handy."

This time Hank wanted to kick himself instead of the door. He'd underestimated Russell. His obsession with insects made him seem harmless.

Hank had a few obsessions of his own like

protecting his family, caring for wounded animals, and never letting anyone hurt Rachel again.

Maybe Russell did love her in his own way. And that might be the key to his freedom. "I know you care about Rachel," he said through the door. "But you don't know anything about me—and I care about her too."

His honesty was greeted with another derisive snort. "Right. If you cared about her, you would have let me stay with her to protect her from that stalker."

Now Hank was confused. Maybe due to the 3000 volts that had just shot through his body or the possibility that Russell was telling the truth. "Aren't you her stalker?"

"No, you nitwit. I mailed her love quotes to ease my way back into her life."

Hank closed his eyes, his mind swimming. "If you sent those love quotes, why didn't she recognize your handwriting?"

Russell snorted again. "Because women love a mystery. I gave some of my insect collection to a fellow entomologist in exchange for him writing those quotes. That's how you know it's real love."

Hank didn't know what to say that. So instead he pounded on the door with both fists. "Just let me out of here."

"So you can put your own spin on it? No way,

Holden. You cowboys can make a woman believe anything."

"You can't keep me away from her forever," Hank countered, looking frantically around the closet for a hairpin so he could pick the lock.

"I don't need forever. I'm going over to her place right now to tell her the truth. By the time I'm through, she'll never speak to you again."

Hank started digging through storage boxes, throwing old work clothes and a canteen on the floor around him and tipping over the thermos of coffee. Small drops of coffee seeped through a crack in the lid, soaking into the cover of a book entitled, *The Wonderful World of Insects*.

"She won't take you back, Baker," Hank shouted, "no matter how she feels about me. So if this is some ploy to win her heart, it's going to backfire on you." He heard heavy footsteps on the other side of the door, then the distinct sound of car keys.

"I know it's probably over between Rachel and me," Russell said, sounding resigned. "We can't ever go back. But I'm going to give it one more shot because I still care about her."

Hank was running out of options and out of ideas. He couldn't stay cooped up in this closet while Russell set out to ruin his life. "Wait...you can't just leave me in here. I'm...claustrophobic. I'll go nuts."

Russell emitted an unsympathetic chuckle. "You

should see a therapist about that problem. I'll ask Rachel if she can recommend one. See ya, Holden." Then he was gone.

Rachel's hand hurt from pounding so long on Hank's front door, but she wasn't about to go away. Lights blazed inside the house, so she knew he was hiding somewhere inside. A typical coward. She'd stand out here until the sun came up if necessary. Finally she heard footsteps, then the front door opened.

Russell blinked at her in surprise. "Rachel?"

"Hello, Russell. Hank really needs to get a door-bell. In fact, I think I'll tell him that in person. Along with a few other things." She stepped inside and looked around. "Where is he?"

He swallowed, his Adam's apple bobbing in his throat. "Hank? Well, um, this really isn't a good time."

"Don't tell me you're defending him? You're my ex-fiancé; you're supposed to be on my side."

"I am on your side, Lovebug. I've always been on your side. That's why..." He licked his lips and looked nervously toward the staircase.

Rachel headed in that direction. "He's hiding upstairs?" That didn't sound like the Hank she'd come to know, but she never thought he'd stand her up for their dinner date either.

"He's not exactly hiding," Russell said, heading her off before she could climb up the stairs. "We need to talk."

She heard a rumbling from above, then Hank's booming shout. "Get me out of here!"

Russell gulped, looking more nervous than she'd ever seen him. He raked his long fingers through his thick blond hair. "About Hank..."

"What about him?" Rachel asked, prickles of uneasiness crawling down her spine. "What's going on here, Russell?"

He took a deep breath. "Holden locked himself in a closet and I can't find the key. I've looked every-where. I was just going out for a locksmith when you arrived. He's getting a little...hysterical."

That didn't sound like Hank either.

She pushed past Russell, taking the steps two at a time. She followed the sound of Hank's hoarse shouts until she reached a big bedroom on the west side of the house. It contained a full-size bed with a white wrought-iron headboard a maple chest of drawers, and a man in the closet.

Rachel moved to the closet door, twisting the brass knob, but it wouldn't budge. "Hank?"

"Rachel?"

The way he said her name made her tingle all

the way down to her toes. His voice was full of relief and hope and some other undefinable emotion.

"Rachel, your buggy fiancé is cracking up. He locked me in here."

"Ex-fiancé," Rachel amended as Russell walked into the bedroom. "And why would he lock you in the closet?"

Russell make a cuckoo motion, circling one finger around his ear. "The guy is delirious. He told me he's claustrophobic."

"Hank, are you claustrophobic?" Rachel shouted through the door.

"Of course not!" he exclaimed. "Let's get this straight once and for all. I'm not claustrophobic, I'm not impotent, and I'm not making this up. Just look for Russell's taser."

His taser? Rachel looked at Russell. He shrugged and shook his head as he held out his empty hands. And she didn't see anything that looked like a taser in the room. Maybe Hank was claustrophobic because he sounded a little irrational.

"Hank, just relax," she called in her most soothing, professional tone. "Take slow, even breaths and imagine you're in a cocoon."

"I've never been in a cocoon," he replied, sounding more frustrated than ever. "But I have been stuck in this musty old closet for the last hour. That's why I missed our date. Russell is trying to protect you from me."

Russell sighed. "The guy might look like a stud, but I think he's nuts. And probably needs a psychiatric evaluation. Should I call the paramedics?"

Rachel jumped as she heard the sound of Hank's fist hitting the door.

"Drop the act, Baker," Hank growled. "We both know you locked me in here after you tasered me. You also admitted to mailing those love quotes to Rachel. And bartered with another entomologist so she wouldn't recognize the handwriting."

Rachel looked at Russell. He tugged at his shirt collar and gave her a shaky smile. "What a wild imagination. Why would I do something like that? It's crazy."

"Because" Hank bellowed, "you're broke. You might still love Rachel, but you love money more. I talked to Lee and found out you've been in Texas for weeks, maybe longer. Even did chores on her farm to earn extra cash."

Rachel looked at Russell. "Did you even go to Africa?"

"Of course I did," he retorted. "I got lost too, then had to use all my money finding my way back to you. That's when I knew I couldn't live without you."

Rachel's eyes blurred as she looked up at Russell. "Unlock the door."

He folded his arms across his chest, his jaw set in a stubborn line. "I don't have the key."

"Russell," she said, patient with him, because her heart was full of love, "please open the door."

Russell hesitated. "Do you love him?"

She bit her lip and nodded.

"Hey, Baker," Hank suddenly called out. "I have a question. Is a yellow bug with little red spots all over it considered poisonous?"

Russell perked up. "You don't mean a *Anthrenus scrophulariae,* do you?"

"I'm not sure," Hank replied. "There's one crawling in here on the floor. I'll step on it, then shove it under the door so you can take a look."

"No," Russell shrieked, diving for the door as he pulled a key out of his pocket. "Don't touch it!" He twisted the key in the lock until it clicked and the door came open. The next moment he lay flat out on the floor, courtesy of Hank's fist.

"You were right, Baker." Hank dropped a thick entomology tome on Russell's chest. "This book did come in handy."

Then he walked up to Rachel "How come I'm the one hired to protect you, but you're always rescuing me?"

"You're just lucky, I guess."

"You got that right." He put on his suit coat. "And I owe you a dinner."

She smiled. "And I'll take you up on it. Bonnie's Diner is open all night. Then I have plenty of time to explain how I caught my stalker."

"What?" he asked in surprise.

"Georgie helped me. Buy me some pancakes and I'll tell you all about it."

"You've got a deal."

The next evening, Hank arrived at Rachel's house to pick up his dog. Now that she was out of danger, Rachel didn't need the protection of him or Georgie anymore. And while Hank was glad about it, he was going miss spending time with her.

"These are for you," he told her, placing two bottles of blackberry cordial on her kitchen counter, "courtesy of Grandma Hattie. They're her customer appreciation gifts."

Rachel sat on a kitchen barstool, catching up on paperwork from the clinic. "But Molly and Gina hired you, so they should get the cordial."

He grinned. "You might want to taste it before you start giving it away."

She closed the folder in front of her and smiled. "Maybe I will."

Despite everything that had happened yesterday, he still felt an odd tension between them. They'd ended the night as friends, with Rachel giving him a chaste kiss on the cheek. He really couldn't blame her after all she'd been through with Russell and Dr. Craig. Two men she'd admired and trusted had betrayed her. So it might take a while for her to heal.

And Hank was willing to wait.

"I heard from Luke Rafferty," he told hr. "Sounds like Dr. Craig is going to officially retire and, as part of his plea agreement, he's also paying some big fines and has to attend mandatory counseling."

She nodded. "I heard that too. He's also selling his fourth of the ownership of Craig Clinic to Noah, Jenna, and me at half the cost. He does feel very badly about what happened."

"He should," Hank said harshly, remembering what the man put Rachel through.

She nodded. "I truly don't think he meant to hurt me. I just wish it had turned out differently."

"Well, if it makes you feel better, Russell has a new job."

She raised a quizzical brow. "Where did you hear that?"

"Lee called me. She's got a cell phone and I'm her emergency contact for whenever Sassy needs vet care." He sighed. "I'm going to be seeing a lot of that mule in my future. And so is Russell. He's doing chores for Lee and helping around her cabin. That's how he's going to pay her back for stealing her red

Buick. And what will keep her from pressing charges as long as he keeps up his side of the bargain."

"At least he gets to stay out of jail." Rachel swirled on the barstool to face him. "I feel like I just got out of jail, although I'm really going to miss Georgie."

"I'm sure she'll miss you too." Hank wanted to say more, but something held him back. He'd never been this reticent around a woman before, so he didn't know what was wrong with him. Maybe it was just another side effect of his concussion.

"Georgie has been acting a little strangely today," Rachel said, her brow furrowed. "I'm worried about her. "Every time I've gone near her this afternoon, she runs away from me."

Hank smiled. "I think I might know the problem." Then he whistled. "Georgie, come here, girl."

The dog dashed over to him, her brown ears flying.

"Sit," he commanded and waited until the dog dutifully obeyed before he leaned down to gently pry open her mouth. Then he reached in and pulled out a very soggy anklet sock. "I forgot to tell you that Georgie's a sock thief. No matter how much I've trained her, she just can't resist a sock when she sees one."

"She eats socks?" Rachel asked in amazement. "I had no idea."

He chuckled. "No, she's never actually eaten one.

She just likes to carry it around inside her mouth like a trophy. And if anyone comes near her, she thinks they're going to take it away from her, so she runs."

Rachel slid off the barstool. "I folded laundry over an hour ago, so she must have snatched my sock then." Amusement flashed in her green eyes. "Are you telling me it's been in her mouth that long?"

"Yes, she's very stealth about it. She really loves socks."

"Oh, sweet Georgie," Rachel said, laughing as she turned toward the dog. "Do you want a treat?"

Georgie raced through the open archway that led into the kitchen and stared at the treat jar on the counter, prancing with anticipation until Rachel fed her a couple of crunchy canine cookies. Then she bent down to pet her. "Such a good girl," she told the dog. "So smart and adorable."

Hank watched Georgie lap up the attention. "Are you're saying she's a lot like me?"

Rachel gave him a wry smile. "I'm not sure adorable is the right word to describe you."

"Then what word would you choose?"

Rachel straightened and started walking toward him. "Strong. Handsome. Witty." As she drew closer, the mood between them suddenly shifted into something more electric. "Stubborn. Bullheaded. Obstinate."

"Those last three all mean the same thing."

"Exactly." She looked up at him. "I've learned you're a man who knows what he wants and will stop at nothing to get it, no matter what it costs you." She reached out one hand and placed it lightly on his chest, right over his heart. "You love so deeply that you put everyone else ahead yourself."

"Is this Rachel the therapist talking?" he asked huskily. "Or Rachel the woman?"

"Rachel the friend." She slowly slid her hand up his chest and around the back of his neck. "But what if I want more than that?"

Hank didn't move, his body tensing. Some part of his brain shouted at him to run—that she was about to breach the walls he'd been building around his heart since he was eleven years old. The walls that protected him from ever being hurt or vulnerable again.

Protected him or imprisoned him? For the first time, Hank wanted to know the difference.

"Then show me," he said, wrapping his arms around her.

So she did.

His reticence faded away as she moved her full, soft lips over his mouth. Then she deepened the kiss and he pulled her close, pouring his heart and soul into her. Forgetting everything but how right she felt in his arms.

When they finally broke the kiss, she stared up at

him, flushed and breathless. "That felt...like you really meant it."

"I did." He tenderly brushed a delicate red curl from her brow. "For the first time in my life, I kissed a woman I'm madly in love with."

She leaned up on her toes to plant tender, featherlight kisses along his jaw.

"What do you think, Georgie?" she asked playfully between kisses. "Does he love me?"

But strangely, the dog didn't appear at the sound her name. That's when Hank realized Georgie was nowhere in sight.

"Where'd she go?" Rachel asked, her gaze scanning the living room.

"She's disappeared." Holding Rachel close to him, he looked around the floor. "And so has the sock. I must have dropped it when I realized I've fallen in love with you."

"Good for her." Rachel smiled up at him, her eyes shining. "She ran off with the love of her life. And I'm in the arms of mine."

Don't miss the next book in this five-book series, *Cowboy Bounty Hunter*.

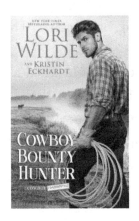

Dear Reader,

Thank you so much for reading *Cowboy Protector*. If you enjoyed Hank and Rachel's story, we would so appreciate a review. You have no idea how much it means to us!

If you'd like to keep up with our latest releases, you can sign up for Lori's newsletter @ https://loriwilde.com/subscribe/

Or follow Lori on Bookbub. https://www.bookbub.com/profile/lori-wilde

To check out other books, you can visit us on the web @ www.loriwilde.com.

Much love and light!

—Lori & Kristin

ABOUT THE AUTHORS

Kristin Eckhardt is the author of 49 novels with over two million copies sold worldwide. She is a two-time RITA award winner who loves writing romantic fiction. Her debut novel was made into a television movie called Recipe for Revenge. After earning a degree in Animal Science, Kristin and her husband raised three children on a farm on the Nebraska prairie. Along with writing, she enjoys baking, sewing, and spending time with family and friends.

Lori Wilde is the New York Times, USA Today and Publishers' Weekly bestselling author of 96 works of romantic fiction. She's a three time Romance Writers' of America RITA finalist and has four times been nominated for Romantic Times Readers' Choice Award. She has won numerous other awards as well.

Her books have been translated into 26 languages, with more than five million copies of her books sold worldwide.

Her breakout novel, *The First Love Cookie Club*,

has been optioned for a TV movie along with the first book in her *Wedding Veil Wishes* series.

Lori is a registered nurse with a BSN from Texas Christian University and holds a certificate in forensics.

A fifth generation Texan, Lori lives with her husband, Bill, in the Cutting Horse Capital of the World.

Made in the USA
Monee, IL
10 March 2021

62372630R00146